THE BAT WOMAN

BRUIN ASYLUM NO. 7

THE BAT WOMAN

CROMWELL GIBBONS

BRUIN BOOKS

PLUS ULTRA

The Bat Woman
©1938 by Cromwell Gibbons

Edited by Jonathan Eeds
Cover design by Michelle Policicchio
Original cover art image provided by

Additional thanks to Mark Terry of Facsimile Dust Jackets LLC for supplying the first
edition dust jacket image of THE BAT WOMAN. Mark's website can be found at
www.facsimiledustjackets.com

This book was crafted in the USA but is printed globally

Printed in the USA
ISBN 978-0-9987065-1-1
Published June, 2017
Bruin Books, LLC
Eugene, Oregon, USA

THE BAT WOMAN

Our story begins . . .

1

THE FINE, driven snow beat in whistling gusts against the lofty windows of the Explorers Club. In the rambling oak-paneled lounge lined with bookcases, above which were murals and geographical charts, isolated groups sat at ease in deeply cushioned leather chairs, their subdued conversation scarcely rising above a hum. In the wide alcove snugly recessed from the frosted bay windows the mounted heads of polar bear, leopard, hippopotamus—trophies from the Arctic to the Tropics—looked down upon four large ruddy men lounging in club chairs around a low table, on which stood two bottles of whisky and a seltzer siphon.

Colonel Hadlow Winthrop, the African big-game sportsman, had just finished speaking. A well-preserved man, gray-haired and with a meticulously groomed Vandyke beard, he was the embodiment of dignity as he sat back with a perplexed frown.

Makonjie, the mouse-hued parrot—the Club's pet from the Congo—was perched in the open room on a branch. Blandly indifferent to the howling storm without, he inquisitively cocked his head at the group and punctuated the stillness with a shrill screech. The marine clock on the wall sounded eight bells.

The Colonel stirred slightly in his chair, cleared his throat importantly. Well, gentlemen, he went on at length, his stern gray eyes casually resting on a large globe of the world, his voice betraying emotion, our man should be here presently. I particularly want you, Dr. Hampden and Captain Sheldon, to tell him of your little encounter with this fellow Schalkenbach. What you have to say I'm sure will be of considerable importance to Professor Huxford.

Sprawled in his chair with his leg hooked over its leather arm, Thornton Hopewell, journalist and citizen of the world, smiled cynically across to the Colonel.

"I call it tommyrot," he said. "Your son's story sounds like the weird concoction of a reefer smoker. Looks like a case for a psychiatrist rather than a problem for a criminologist like your friend Professor Huxford."

"Nonsense!" retorted the Colonel. "I disagree with you entirely. Thornton-Robert doesn't go in for that sort of thing. He isn't a neurotic, and I haven't the slightest reason to doubt him."

"And you're sure he hadn't been overindulging?"

"I am," the Colonel replied with certainty. "Of course,

he takes an occasional one, but I've never known him to drink to excess. Somehow, I can't believe this was an hallucination."

Captain Steven Sheldon, the famous South American explorer and lecturer, drew on his large calabash pipe and pensively blew puffs of smoke.

"At least there can't be any doubt about the existence of this man Schalkenbach," he remarked. "He was a man you could never forget once you had seen him. But what on earth would he be doing with your son's wife, assuming, for the sake of argument, that it was she?"

"Anyway," said the journalist with a chuckle, "even if she's supposed to be dead, why should such a girl jeopardize her position in society? What would she be doing in company with this grotesque mug? Why, hell! Such doings would be an insult to the most holy pages of the Social Register, don't you—"

"That's just the point, Thornton, interrupted the Colonel. I'm afraid you don't quite understand. If Cynthia is really alive—which I cannot believe—their being together is more credible than you might think. Schalkenbach once greatly admired Cynthia, and for a time she seemed to be attracted by him."

"Preposterous," the journalist scoffed, leaning toward the table and helping himself to a straight whisky. "How could Robert be so sure in a large auditorium like the Metropolitan?" He gulped down his drink and added, "I wonder how close he was to them."

"It's all very perplexing," declared the Colonel. "But,

I'm determined to get to the bottom of this thing. There's more to it than mere fantasy."

"I can understand," mused the journalist, "Robert's seeing this fabulous person Schalkenbach at the opera. But when you suggest the fantastic idea of a dead and buried woman rising from the grave to join this creature . . . Damn it to hell! That sounds crazy—and calls for another drink."

"I'm inclined to agree with you, Colonel." The Reverend Percival Hampden, a missionary lately arrived from Borneo, was speaking. "At least, something should be done to put Robert's mind at ease. Can you tell us anything about him that might be helpful?"

The Colonel wrinkled his brow in thought.

"My boy is quiet and enjoys things in moderation," he replied after a moment's silence. "He early showed an unusual interest in business, which was very gratifying to me. It has been my observation that an enterprise which succeeds for more than a generation has two hurdles to surmount. I have long felt that to find someone to carry on a successful business is even more difficult than to endure the hardships involved in starting one. In that respect," he ended, with a note of pride in his voice, "Robert has fulfilled my expectations and is successfully carrying on the family business.

"I admit I was a little surprised at the girl he fell in love with—she was so much his opposite. She dabbled in the arts—painting, I believe. Cynthia was inclined to be Bohemian, went in for the exotic. Before their engagement she spent much time in the Latin Quarter of Paris and in Budapest."

The missionary folded his arms. "I vividly recall their wedding at the Little Church around the Corner," he said in his well-modulated voice. "It was on the eve of my sailing for South America to establish a mission post in the land of the Jivaros—the head-hunters." He paused, his deep-set black eyes looking straight ahead. "I can see her now," he went on reflectively. "Her slender figure in a white flowing gown, and her radiant black eyes and jet-black hair. She was a classic beauty." He shook his head slowly. "Her early death must have been a great blow to Robert."

"By the way," asked Hopewell, "where did she meet this strange person?"

"It was on the *Bremen*," the Colonel replied. "It was shortly before her engagement when she was returning from Europe. He was very attentive to her on the ship. While he was in New York, he was a frequent visitor at the Hargrave home, according to Robert. What Cynthia saw in this man Schalkenbach we could none of us understand. But she had always been intrigued by the bizarre. Perhaps it was this that attracted her. Robert is so conservative. In fact, as I intimated before, I was astonished when her engagement to him was announced."

Captain Sheldon drank his whisky and soda, and looked quizzically at the Colonel. "You say it was last week at the Metropolitan that you son says he saw his wife?"

"Yes. It was at a performance of *Die Meistersinger*. It has become an obsession with my boy. If something isn't done soon, I'm afraid he's headed for a breakdown."

"Come, come, Colonel," twitted the journalist, "I trust you're not sharing Robert's hallucination! By the way, did you ever meet this fellow Schalkenbach?"

"Frankly," the Colonel admitted, I've never met this extraordinary man. What I've learned about him has come entirely through my son, Captain Sheldon and Dr. Hampden.

"Has Professor Huxford agreed to take the case?" asked Captain Sheldon.

"I had a brief chat with him about it at the Yale Club," the Colonel replied. "He seemed interested, and made the appointment to meet us here. He's a man who can be relied upon to look into the matter with the utmost discretion. I shouldn't want to have it aired in the newspapers."

"Then let me tell you about this sleuth, Rex Huxford," remarked the journalist dryly. "I agree that he's a discreet chap, quiet and unassuming—and all that sort of thing. But the very fact he's on a case is sure to attract the press. Look what happened to Abe Goldsmith. He hired the Professor because he thought the police would bungle the death of William Whalen and there'd be unfavorable publicity. The laugh is that the unsuspecting coroner would have passed the famous director's death as an acute heart attack, but Huxford stepped in and proved it to be murder—much to the satisfaction of the newspapers and the chagrin of Goldsmith."

The missionary turned his gaunt tanned face toward Hopewell. "Doubt and condemnation without first seeking the truth are the scourge of the soul, he stated solemnly, emphasizing each word. Things do happen under heaven and on earth—strange, uncanny, mystifying things . . . sometimes born of evil. But let us first seek the truth. For truth is the wisdom—"

"Pardon me, sir, interrupted the Colonel, rising from his chair, hut here is Professor Huxford."

2

REX HUXFORD, a slenderly built man of forty with dark hair and clean-cut features, shed his snow-flaked overcoat into the hands of a nimble attendant. He wore loosely fitting tweeds and carried a Malacca cane, which he hung over his arm as he strode into the lounge.

"Nasty weather to get one out," apologized the Colonel, shaking hands with the criminologist.

"Not at all, Colonel, not in the least," he replied, smiling. "I took a cab and came straight across Central Park."

A Negro attendant in a spotless white coat rushed to get Huxford a chair.

"Right here, sir, yessir, yessir," he said, bowing repeatedly.

The formalities over, Huxford, holding on to his cane, settled into the chair. Colonel Winthrop turned to the alert Negro attendant.

"Here, Zipp!" he ordered. "Bring us a fresh siphon of seltzer."

"Yessir, Colonel, yessir," he replied, his broad white teeth flashing as he backed away with the tray.

"Your son, I presume," Huxford asked, smiling faintly, "is still shocked over his curious experience at the opera?"

The Colonel raised his eyebrows. "Yes, he's quite upset. He can't sleep, he tells me. When I spoke to him of your interest in the matter he brightened up—it seemed to relieve his mind."

The journalist turned to Huxford. "The young man sure has plenty of reason to be disturbed," he remarked with an amused smile. "Imagine a man's embarrassment at seeing the ghost of his wife! It's so preposterous." He chuckled. "What do you think of it, Professor Huxford?"

"I would rather not venture an opinion, I know so little about the matter."

Captain Sheldon leaned forward and took out his tobacco pouch. "There's one certainty, at least," he declared, as he loaded his pipe, "the fellow Schalkenbach. I'm sure Dr. Hampden and I can attest to his reality."

"Yes," Huxford nodded, toying with his cane, "I understand that after leaving your Brazilian expedition Dr. Hampden had a later encounter with him in the East Indies. I should like to hear more about this man from both of you."

The missionary looked up solemnly. "A psychoanalysis of this pitiable monstrosity," he remarked pompously, "should reveal much light concerning the motivation of the unholy creature, who I fear has strayed from the path of God to conspire with the Devil."

"Perhaps Captain Sheldon will tell his story first," the Colonel suggested. "I'm sure Professor Huxford will learn a good deal from what you have to say."

The explorer lighted his pipe and settled back in his chair.

"It was on my second expedition to the Amazon country," he began impressively. "We had made the uneventful voyage to Para, and the long journey up the Amazon to Manaos. Here we stopped to engage Indian porters for the boat trip up the Madeira and the hazardous trek into the unexplored land of the head-hunters. The purpose of our expedition was to collect specimens of Indian life and learn, if possible, from the cannibals, the closely guarded secret of their method of shrinking heads.

"While stopping over at Manaos I had the good fortune to meet Dr. Hampden. He was planning to establish a mission post on the frontier of Ecuador, a wild unexplored section west of the jungle territory my expedition hoped to penetrate. It seemed natural for us to combine forces, and I invited him to join us. Hampden's knowledge of Indian life proved invaluable. Had it not been for his tact and the friendly way he handled the savages, I don't doubt in the least that our heads would now be prize examples of the ghastly art of headshrinking."

He paused and blew a ring of smoke.

"We had left by way of Manaos, going down the Amazon to Mara, an outpost near the junction of the Madeira River," he went on in the formal delivery of the lecturer. "From Mara, we navigated the treacherous Madeira into the heart of a forest seen by few white men . . . We faced the unpleasant fact that the river was full of hungry crocodiles snapping their brutal jaws at our very shadows.

"Along the river at a clearing we were able to trade with some of the more friendly savages. For the equivalent of five dollars we managed to procure a shrunken head and a splendid example of a reduced and mummified human body. Our specimen of a whole body, in my opinion, is as good as the two in the Museum of American Indian History. Here in the cabinet is one of the unfortunate old conquistadors." Pausing, he turned toward the cabinet.

"This gentleman," he explained, pointing with his pipe to a puttylike doll figure of a man which was suspended by its long black hair, "was searching for El Hombre Dorado, the golden man, when he was captured by the head-hunters and reduced from a living man of five feet nine inches to a shrunken mummy only twenty-one inches tall."

"I note that his lips are sealed by a tassel," remarked Huxford.

"That's a superstition of the headhunter," the Captain pointed out, "a part of the savage's religious rite. It is done to prevent his victim from talking." He settled back in his chair.

"It was while at this clearing, just before we entered the unexplored jungle," he continued, "that we came upon the old renegade Pat Morgan. That red-bearded, blustering, swashbuckling soldier of fortune was leading a band of nondescript adventurers. Morgan and his armed-to-the-teeth cutthroats were going after platinum, which was

said to be a common commodity among the mountain savages. He had very definite ideas as to a short cut through
the jungle to this El Dorado. We wished him luck. Then we
took a course up the unexplored branch of the river, which
snaked westward into a dense tropical maze of giant trees
and vines—"

"By the way," interrupted Hopewell, "did this adven-
turer Pat Morgan find his haven of easy gold?"

"No one saw or heard of him again. But three months
later when I returned to the spot, a shrunken and mummified head with a red beard and red hair was offered for
sale."

"Huh . . . !" grunted the journalist.

Captain Sheldon paused, knocked out his pipe, and
loaded it. "Traveling in a virgin forest can never be a wholly
pleasant experience," he went on, "but when the forest lies
along the bank of a river within a few degrees of the equa-
tor, a day's journey often becomes a long drawn out ordeal,
with mud, steaming heat, insects like caterpillars that suck
one's blood, deadly serpents that hang overhead and crawl
under foot, wild beasts that howl in the night, and dense
vegetation—all acting in concert to take the heart out of the
invader and bid him turn back.

"We had halted in the late afternoon, since it was customary to make an early start in the morning—in a low
equatorial country the first few hours of the day are usually
worth all the others put together. I had taken the sextant
to shoot the sun when my attention was suddenly arrested
by the most terrifying bellowing I had ever heard. It was

like the guttural wailing of some monstrous beast in an agonized struggle, crying out for its life. We peered about but could not see anything for the jungle. This uncanny disturbance was immediately followed by a great splash in the river and a turbulent swishing of the water.

"Dr. Hampden and I and my Indian gunbearer hastily but cautiously beat our way along the densely vegetated bank of the river. Scarcely two hundred yards ahead, we came upon the cause of the commotion. A twenty-foot crocodile was violently churning and slapping the foaming water with thunderous claps. The monstrous brute leaped and fell, and with each mighty lash of its powerful scaly tail shot huge sheets of water high into the air. This was not an alligator, you understand, but the more dangerous crocodile. It was the largest mugger any of us had ever seen, a man-eating species. Even in captivity it is untamable—the most vicious reptile known.

"We were even more astonished to see grappling with this giant crocodile a powerful beast, more powerful than anything I had ever dared to imagine—a hairy thing like a gorilla. I had never seen a struggle like it. The thing was straddling the amphibious brute, its muscular arms locking the bucking crocodile's vicious jaw with the grip of a strangler.

"Craftily, the hairy ape worked the battling crocodile into shallow water, where with superhuman effort and the science of a wrestler it bent the grunting mugger's head back until we could see its white quivering belly. This mapped the spine of the giant saurian. It lay paralyzed.

Then the victor tossed the scaly beast to the bank of the river as if it meant nothing. We stood in utter amazement. I knew that the country was not the habitat of the gorilla, but yet here in a jungle seen by white men for the first time was what looked like one. Yet the monstrous thing looked even more like a rugged primitive man—perhaps, a descendant of some prehistoric race like the Neanderthal, a brute species of giant man from the lost world. What was it . . . this creature, hideous beyond belief, that at any moment might spot us and annihilate our puny group?

"I raised my gun and fired a shot high over the beast's bushy head. It bounded around in startled surprise. Its shaggy hair fell away from its face, its eyes flashed with savage rage, and its enormous lips curled into a menacing snarl.

"'Pass auf! Pass auf! Don't shoot, I'm a white man!' the thing bellowed, sticking its chunky hands up.

"We were stupefied. I lowered my gun but kept my finger on the trigger. On he came, in a shuffling, awkward gait, weaving his massive arms fearsomely, the jungle growth giving way before his beastlike bulk.

"'I'm Dr. Eric von Schalkenbach,' the brute announced, towering above us and extending his hand in greeting. 'I apologize if I have caused you alarm. You must forgive my unkempt appearance.'"

3

REX HUXFORD sipped his drink and replaced it on the table. "Did this Dr. Schalkenbach explain," he asked, leaning back, "why he was living in the jungle like a savage?"

The explorer nodded to the missionary. "I believe Dr. Hampden can best answer that question," he said.

"Yes and no," the missionary replied hesitantly. "Dr. Schalkenbach, despite his regrettable abnormality, was a man of surprising intelligence and education—an unfortunate who I dare say had abandoned the cultured world to revel in the jungles like a savage, in utter contempt of civilization and God. I recall his remarks the night when we were alone at the dinner table.

"'What chance have I,' he confided to me, leaning his huge form over the table, 'with a face like this, to practice an honorable profession?' He smiled scornfully at a table knife he was bending between his fingers. 'My birth was a horrible mistake,' he said bitterly. 'A man that doesn't belong . . . a magnanimous intelligence imprisoned in a hideous carcass ... a misfit. I only frighten—'"

"Pew!" half-whistled the journalist. "What a wrestler he'd make! Imagine a King Kong like that battling for the world's championship at the Garden."

Passing over the remark, Huxford turned to the missionary. "And what did you learn about his parentage, Dr. Hampden?" he asked.

"Not a solitary thing," the missionary replied. "He was sulky and evasive about his past. We did not even learn how he managed to live in the jungle. The Indians we met indicated that they knew him but were reluctant to give us information. They showed considerable reverence for this intellectual brute, this king of the jungles. In fact, I believe, he so impressed them that they worshiped him as a strange white god. His skill and superhuman strength in subduing giant crocodiles no doubt accounts in part for their worship.

"How long did he stay with your party?"

"He left us before daylight. No one heard him go." He paused. "I believe Colonel Winthrop knows about his parentage."

"I understand he was born in Düsseldorf," the Colonel replied, "and specialized in surgery at Heidelberg."

"Did Dr. Schalkenbach tell you so?"

"Indeed no! As I stated before, I never saw the man. I was away at the time. It was Cynthia he confided in, prior to her marriage to my son."

"Are you sure he told her nothing else of importance?"

"If he did, she kept it to herself."

"I take it Dr. Schalkenbach was keenly interested in anthropology. Did he say anything about the shrinking and mummifying of human heads?"

"He seemed to be an authority on the subject," Captain Sheldon answered. "The only authentic information we have came through him. As a matter of fact, the process had remained a mystery for many years. I believe Dr.

Schalkenbach is the only white man ever to witness the process and live to tell its secrets. He also boasted that he had successfully performed among the savages surgical operations without the aid of the usual anesthetics, inducing a state of anesthesia by hypnosis."

"So he is a hypnotist too!" remarked the Journalist sardonically.

Huxford smiled faintly, and twirled his cane. "The hypnotic method of inducing general anesthesia is not new," he said. "It's of German origin. It has been successfully practiced by only a skilled few. But I'd like to hear what he had to say about the shrinking of human heads."

The explorer stretched his legs and lit his pipe. As soon as a headhunter kills an enemy, he hacks off the head as close as possible to the body, and carries it away to a secluded place," he explained. "Here he goes through a weird mumbo-jumbo ceremony, working himself up to a savage frenzy.

"He slits the scalp from the crown to the nape of the neck. Through the opening he scrapes out the skull, then stretches the skin over a ball-like handle made of wood and thrusts it for ten minutes into a vessel of boiling water causing it to shrink. Next a ring fashioned from a vine is sewn in the opening of the neck to keep it from closing, when hot stones are dropped inside. The head is then filled with hot sand and kept in constant motion in order that the sand may act uniformly on all parts of the head. As the sand cools it is reheated and put back in the head. The inside is scraped each time with a headman's knife to remove the burnt tissues. As the head dries and grows smaller the Indian works the features with his hand, pinching and molding the face so that it will retain its natural appearance—and even its natural expression when reduced several times."

"The process would seem to embody some of the ancient Egyptian's secrets of mummifying," commented Huxford.

"I wouldn't be surprised if this Dr. Schalkenbach knew more than he told."

"Do you think that he was in the Amazon country just to learn to shrink heads?" the Colonel questioned.

"It's quite probable he was engaged in some biological work. I can't believe his sole object in subduing a vicious crocodile was merely to get its hide. It may interest you to know that a number of our eminent medical authorities agree that the conclusions from study of the brain, the thyroid gland, and other vital parts of wild animals may have a bearing on the life span of man. It's unfortunate, Captain Sheldon, that you didn't take a look at the crocodile the next morning."

"But I don't see the connection," said the explorer.

"It wouldn't have surprised me in the least," explained Huxford, "if you had found that the crocodile had been dissected and the vital organs carefully removed. The snapping of its spine merely paralyzed it. It offered an unusual opportunity for our dexterous field surgeon to obtain its organs while the beast was still alive."

"That probably accounts for his stealing away before

dawn," declared the missionary, his eyes brightening.

"Precisely!" stated Huxford.

"Perhaps the old buzzard was after a magic elixir," bantered the journalist. "But can you explain such a freak of nature," he asked in a more serious tone, addressing Huxford, "a prodigy like this Dr. Schalkenbach?"

"Genetics—nature's rigorous law of heredity," the criminologist replied in a quiet tone of authority, "the organic relation between generations. Through successive generations there persists a constancy of likeness or stability of type. But in many cases the offspring exhibit not only parental but also ancestral characteristics and in exceptional cases they revert to their primitive ancestors—these are called reversions, or throwbacks. In the case of Schalkenbach, I venture to say that we have a classic example of a throwback to the primeval age of the giant gorilla like man."

"Then you contend, like Darwin, that man sprang from the ape?" questioned the journalist.

"Darwin did not claim that man sprang from the ape, but that both were derived from a common anthropoid ancestor."

"And you believe in the evolutionary theory of species?"

Huxford smiled benignly. "A scientific mind could hardly believe otherwise." Bending his cane over his knee, he went on: "Structures in the body which are used tend to develop further, and those which are not used tend to disappear. In man's body there're about seventy vestigial structures which were in use in some primitive state. Of course," and he smiled with amusement, "you are all quite aware, no doubt, of the fact that we still have at the base of our spine the remnant structure of a tail."

"That reminds me," remarked Hopewell, the journalist, "of the famous Scopes 'monkey trial' at Dayton. You remember how the late William Jennings Bryan battled in the sweltering heat to save the sovereign State of Tennessee from the evil teaching of evolution, and Clarence Darrow, the hated opponent of the Fundamentalist—well," and he grinned, "I covered that trial and, believe it or not, within the very shadows of the old Court House, was born a boy with a six-inch tail."

"Ironical enough," agreed Huxford, "but you'd be surprised to know the number of like cases recorded in the annals of medical science."

"Did this freak survive?" the Colonel asked.

"Oh, yes," replied the journalist. "The tail was amputated in great secrecy and the affair immediately hushed up."

Captain Sheldon made a loud sucking-noise on his calabash. He cleared his throat and spat at a cuspidor, fashioned out of an elephant's foot.

"I once knew the case of a white woman of good moral standing who gave birth to a black child," he added. "It was a boy with all the physical characteristics of the African race. The affair was disgracefully aired in court. The irate husband vociferously disclaimed parenthood of the child, insisting his wife must have had adulterous relations with

an unknown Negro. Scientific experts and medical authorities were called in, and finally a quiet-working genealogist
traced the parentage of both wife and husband. It was
revealed that on the husband's side, three generations
back, there had occurred a scandalous marriage with a mu-
latto woman, and that the pair had a male child. The able
defense satisfied the jury that there had been no adultery
in this case and that the birth of the black child was a
throwback."

"The credulity of the human race is certainly amazing,"
the journalist scoffed, shaking his head.

The Reverend Dr. Hampden looked across to the journalist. "For I the Lord thy God am a jealous God, visiting
the iniquity of the fathers upon the children unto the third
and fourth generation," solemnly quoted the missionary.

Huxford nodded. "I venture to say, further," he
replied, holding his lighter to his cigarette, "that this Dr.
Schalkenbach's birth was the result of inbreeding. It's a
biological fact that the offspring from blood marriages
sometimes result in monstrosities, and often in idiots
which bear marked resemblance to the ape. Inbreeding
heightens the throwback tendency."

"I feel confident," the Captain said, turning to Huxford, "that what Dr. Hampden has to tell about his later
experience will throw much more light on the man."

"I'm convinced," the missionary remarked, slowly
shaking his head, "that this brute and his heathen servant
who boarded our little schooner at Macassar were embarking on some unsavory enterprise."

4

THE wind howled in gusts against the building; the windows rattled. Dr. Hampden unfolded his arms. His gaze shifted from the comfortably seated group to the frosted window near which he sat. Idly he contemplated the driving snow and the isolated workers toiling with their snow-encumbered implements. He turned his gaunt tanned face slowly from the window.

"Thanks to the splendid assistance of Captain Sheldon—" he nodded across to the explorer, who was languidly smoking his calabash—" I was able to complete my missionary work in the Amazon country early and return to New York for a much-needed rest. It was then that I was recalled to my old post in Borneo." He paused and looked reflective, then went on:

"After helping to establish a number of important stations in the East Indies, I was again thankful to be granted leave to return to New York. At the time, I happened to be in the Dutch Celebes at an obscure port settlement by the name of Macassar. Following weary weeks of impatient waiting, a storm-battered two-masted tramp schooner put in and tied up at the ramshackle dock.

"Eager to get out of this insect-infested country, I went at once to bargain with the Captain about passage. He was a broad-shouldered German, barefooted, his clothes in tatters. A red scar cut diagonally across his weather-beaten face, causing his heavy lips to hang open and expose his gums and the black stubs of his teeth. I was curtly informed in no uncertain terms that he was not eager to accept me as a passenger. The *Swift Star*, he said, would set sail from Macassar across the Java Sea to Surabaya, a distance of about 445 miles. He told me that, if he took me, I would be dropped at Surabaya, where connections could be made for Batavia. Once in Batavia, I could get the steamship to San Francisco. I was determined to get away, and finally the Captain agreed to let me have passage.

"I understood Dutch and I assure you it was quite disquieting to learn of the unsavory character of my German skipper. It was just before embarking that I overheard one of the two Colonial officers who put my passport in order remark, *'Ik vertrouw die vryer niet'*. That means 'I don't trust that fellow'—and he meant the Captain. But I did not change my mind."

"What sort of cargo did this tramp schooner take on?" Huxford asked.

"We took on no cargo, we sailed in ballast," Hampden replied. The rum-soaked Captain talked about the Devil's cargo. He would squint at me with his bloodshot eyes and shout into my face, 'Devil's cargo and a sky pilot to guide us safely!' Then, laughing boisterously as if I were the butt of a joke, he would amble away."

The missionary paused, his deep-set black eyes looking straight ahead. "Sometime before noon I went aboard," he went on. "I was quite fatigued and went aft to rest in the shade of the spanker sail and watch the mixed crew of Singhalese, Kaffirs, and other Asiatics make preparations to sail. I had begun to speculate whether I was destined to be the sole passenger on an irregular ship commanded by a Captain whom I felt I couldn't trust, when out of the steaming haze appeared a procession of naked, sweating natives. Bearing a train of heavily laden chests on bamboo poles over their bare shoulders, they slowly trudged aboard.

"Following in the wake of this unexpected pomp was a huge man immaculately clad in spotless white linen, wearing a pith helmet and enormous black sunglasses. Trotting in his steps was an emaciated Chinese with a long black cue and a walrus like mustache, clad in native dress. The massive man in white swaggered aboard and mumbled some orders to the Captain. I gasped in utter amazement. At first I had not recognized him, but beyond the shadow of a doubt the man was Dr. Schalkenbach. There was no mistaking him—"

"How long ago was that?" Huxford broke in.

The missionary paused in thought. "It was a year and five months ago."

"Did he mention the object of his trip?"

"No. He was bitter and sulky and preferred to be alone. I overheard some grumbling between him and the Captain about my presence. When I did broach the subject, he curtly told me to attend to my own damn business. Then he muttered something blasphemous about in quisitive people. The bilious-looking Chinese was introduced as his secretary. He was polite in an Oriental way."

"Did anything unusual happen before your arrival—at Surabaya?"

"Yes," he replied, his eyes brightening. "We'd hardly reached the Sea of Java, having made rapid headway before a steady wind in a choppy sea, when we were suddenly becalmed. The night was pitch-black and the stars stood out like sparkling diamonds in the tropical sky. There was not a breath of air. I had never seen the water so smooth. It was as if an infinite turbulent expanse of unending sea had magically become a silent, frozen lake of glass. Our insignificant ship, a pygmy specter in the boundless ocean, as still as death, seemed held in the center of a great, fathomless void. Surrounding us and coming from the surface of the water was a suffocating vapor, which rose languidly from the placid sea like slowly escaping steam. The silence, the depressing heat, the vapor, made a humid, steaming inferno that was unbearable.

"I climbed into the forecastle saloon, since sleep was impossible. My head felt as if it were going to burst, as if it were in a vacuum. The Chinese, calmly fanning himself, sat at the rickety table, over which hung a foul-smelling lamp. Pronouncing each word separately and distinctly, he greeted me: 'Very bad weather for sailing vessel'. I nodded, sat down, and took my handkerchief to mop the dripping perspiration from my face. The Captain and Dr. Schalkenbach were in the aft cabin looking over some charts. The crew, save those on watch, were stretched out in the forecastle bunks sweltering in a stench of sweat. 'How long have you been with Dr. Schalkenbach?' I asked casually, trying not to betray any curiosity. The Oriental looked at me sharply with, I thought, some suspicion. 'Honorable doctor', he declared after a pause, 'I know long time like humble birds and humble beasts.'

" 'Your master is very strong and kind,' I said, hoping to draw hint out.

" 'Honorable gracious master, friend of all humanity. He very strong and very wise like great Chinese philosopher."

"The Oriental's inscrutable almond eyes looked straight at me. Then, placing his fan carefully on the table, he leaned toward me and drew a long wooden match from a box.

" 'Honorable master never use crude Western weapon,' he whispered, craftily, as he extended the match carefully between his slender fingers. 'Gracious master pick up unfortunate enemy like insignificant match.' He snapped the match in two, picked up his fan, and calmly relaxed in his chair.

" 'Does he not fear God?' I asked with concern.

" 'Honorable, gracious master, like humble servant, worship no God.'

" 'You mean you don't believe in God?' He smiled enigmatically. 'What is your master's destination?' I asked frankly. 'Where rainbow and land meet—there he shall find peace,' was the cryptic reply.

"I was taking out my missionary manual in order to read some passages to the Oriental, a preliminary proce-

dure I usually employ in my attempts to Christianize heathen, when my attention was diverted by the scuffing of
feet on the forward deck. I looked up. In the frame of the
hatchway appeared the scar-faced Captain. 'All hands on
deck and the cook!' he ordered at the top of his lungs.

"A husky Singhalese sailor acting as mate bounded
down the stairs through the forecastle saloon repeating the
Captain's orders. He bolted into the bunk cabin, where the
crew were still asleep. 'All hands on deck!' he roared
savagely. 'All hands on deck!' He bulldozed, struck with his
fists, and kicked out of their bunks the languid, half-naked,
half-dressed men, who scurried up the narrow compan-
ionway like a pack of driven rats.

"I became anxious and went up on deck. The sails
were lowered and quickly made fast. Standing at the starboard foremast shroud, looming against the sky with its
fading stars, like a massive monster, was Schalkenbach.
He bellowed orders from bow to stern as if he had taken
over command. Apprehensively I approached him. 'What's
happened?' I inquired.

"He turned on me contemptuously, his savage lips o-
pening in a snarl. 'The barometer is dropping—a typhoon!'
he snapped, pushing me aside.

"Scarcely had he spoken when I felt my burning face
fanned by a gentle breeze. In the southern horizon, a
mountainous black cloud was rapidly approaching. Swiftly
it came on, a roaring black mass of increasing wind and
rain. A furious sea began to run. It was unbelievable that
water could be so calm one minute and the next so violent.

The crew of half-naked Asiatics staggered in the blasting wind and stinging rain. Driven under the blasphemous orders of the powerful Schalkenbach, they hoisted from the hold of the storm-tossed vessel his heavily laden chests, and made them fast to the midship deck.

"The wind howled and shrieked through the torn rigging and across the storm-swept boat. In the stern, the husky Singhalese mate forced himself against the steering wheel. Helpless, the little vessel tossed about in the raging surf as if it were a mere hell. Schalkenbach, naked to his waist, watched over his ten valued chests. He stood out in the storm like a mammoth hairy ape. 'Lash down all hatches and companionways!' he bellowed, as if defying the furious elements.

"Drenched in hot sea water, I clung desperately to the rail aft. Suddenly the vessel lurched violently. The German skipper came hurtling out of his cabin onto the sea-swept deck. Clutching a bottle, he braced himself against the aft cabin and gulped its contents. With his bare arm, he wiped his scarred face and then beckoned to three Kaffir' sailors. There must have been an understanding between them, for the three immediately sprang to his side. Battered by the hurtling sea which broke over them all, the brawny, barefooted Captain stealthily led the crouching black sailors around the storm-lashed cabin.

"Amidships the Captain peered cautiously about. Dr. Schalkenbach was nowhere to be seen. Motioning to the sailors, the Captain pointed to one of the chests. With drawn sheath knives, the three Kaffirs pounced upon it and cut away the ropes. The Captain threw the lid open and looked in. At that instant the hairy bulk of Schalkenbach loomed near. The lightning flashed. As he towered over the Captain's shoulders, I could see that his bulging eyes burned with savage anger.

" 'So! You know, do you?' he scornfully assailed the startled skipper, raising his hairy arms. The surprised Captain backing away, moved up to the gunwale. With an iron grip, he seized a belaying pin. The naked Kaffirs, brandishing their knives, drew back, squatted on their haunches, and watched like a pack of panthers waiting to spring. Crouching and holding the belaying pin threateningly over his head, the sneering Captain advanced inch by inch in attack upon the weaponless Schalkenbach. 'I'm captain of this vessel—I'll show you!' he boomed out of the corner of his scar-mangled mouth, drawing the club back, his eyes wild with anger. Swiftly, like the stroke of lightning, he brought the solid belaying pin down with a loud skull-cracking thud on the head of Schalkenbach. Apparently unaffected by the assault, the gigantic gorilla-like brute swooped down and seized the Captain with his massive arms. Then, as if handling a mere doll, Schalkenbach swung the body of the amazed man up over his grimacing face and with brute force hurled it into space. So powerful was the thrust that it catapulted the shaggy form of the Captain over the heads of the Kaffirs, who dropped their knives and fled. The Captain's body landed sprawled out on the deck, his bleeding head over in the scuppers. The vessel lurched violently. A towering wave broke over the boat. The vessel came up. I looked. The Captain was gone.

"The intensity of the wind increased. It was utterly impossible for me to cling to the rail any longer. The vessel dived into the raging trough as if she were headed for the bottom of the sea. Then she was tossed up by a mountainous wave with the speed of a roller coaster. Nearly exhausted, I stumbled to the mizzenmast and lashed myself to it. The rain began to fall in torrents. The crew clung desperately to the rigging as the water swirled about them. The thunder was like the continuous roar of a furious barrage. The lightning played all about us, silhouetting the struggling men against the raging sea.

"Hardly had I made myself fast when another wave even more towering than the preceding one broke with terrific force. It was as if the whole of Niagara Falls had suddenly burst upon the vessel. At the helm the Singhalese mate, caught in the whirling force of the water, was torn from the steering wheel and swept out to sea. Adrift without a helmsman, the boat began to swing into the treacherous trough of the typhoon sea. Once trapped broadside between the furious waves, we would capsize. The vessel was sure to be swamped. I felt we were doomed. I held my gold crucifix reverently before the heavenly flashes which seemed to fill the sky with a continuous blaze. Schalkenbach sprang to the stern deck. He seized the oscillating wheel. His half-naked savage bulk faced me. I beckoned for him to join me in a last prayer. A sneering grin broke across his bulbous face as he looked at me contemptuously. As if the wrath of the Lord had retorted with vengeance, a blinding slash of lightening cracked out with a sharp, deafening report. The main topmast came crashing down on the port side.

" 'Won't you pray for the safekeeping of your soul?' I urged, with scarcely the strength to hold the crucifix before his eyes.

" 'To hell with your God-damned religion!' he retorted, shaking his fist defiantly at the tormented elements. 'I'm master of this ship-not God!' he thundered, rising to his full height and bearing down on the wheel with the strength of a giant."

5

MAKON JIE, the parrot, cocked his head, looked quizzically down at the group, and screeched. Huxford shifted in his chair and turned to Dr. Hampden.

"Did this Dr. Schalkenbach abandon the vessel upon arrival at Surabaya?"

"I'm quite sure he didn't," said the missionary. "The typhoon left as suddenly as it came. Our battered vessel, half disabled, with the Captain and five of the crew missing, limped into the port of Surabaya and dropped anchor. I was assisted into the schooner's dory and taken ashore by an Asiatic sailor.

"Towering in the bow of the *Swift Star*, indifferently watching my departure, was the gorilla-like figure of

Schalkenbach. Standing at his side, nonchalantly fanning him-self, a bland expression on his yellow face, was the complacent Chinese. Grouped in back of these two were the remnant of the crew. Silently they stood, a weird tableau of assorted creatures, which like a spectral scene faded into the distance. That was the last I saw of them."

"What was Dr. Schalkenbach's attitude after the storm?"

"He was not inclined to talk and kept to himself."

"What did he have in those chests?" bluntly asked the journalist.

"Your guess should be as good as mine."

"What! You never found out?"

The missionary smiled faintly. "You heard what happened to the skipper when he grew inquisitive," he retorted.

"Did you examine the chests—notice anything of special interest?" asked Huxford.

The missionary paused. "Yes, now that you mention it. Two of the ten chests, which were constructed of thick oak and bound with rope, were perforated with small holes. That puzzled me."

"Was there anything else that aroused your suspicion?"

"I have never mentioned this before, but on several occasions late at night I could have given my oath that I heard a squealing and rustling noise issuing from those boxes. The idea became almost an obsession. Of course, it may have been just the wind blowing through the rigging."

"Indeed, and more strange," the missionary went on, "was the hot night I slept on the bow deck. It must have been sometime after midnight when I was abruptly awakened. I sat upright. Again my attention was arrested by muffled squealing, which appeared to come from the chests on the midship deck, but I could not see them from where I was lying. The sound was clearer than before. It was more like the chirping of small birds. Then there was a scuffling noise and the squealing became louder. Suddenly a terrified scream rent the stillness of the night.

"'No! No! Not that!' I heard a man's voice plead. A dull thud followed—then all was quiet."

"Did you find out the next morning what had happened?"

The missionary looked up, his black eyes lighting. "Why, yes—one of the Kaffirs was missing. He was a strapping sailor. According to Schalkenbach, the African had been seized with a stroke and died. He said the Negro had become delirious. He hoped I hadn't been disturbed . . . I told him I heard nothing."

"Did you see the body?"

"No, it had been consigned to the sea before dawn. I was not called upon to perform the last rites. Now I understand . . ."

"And Dr. Schalkenbach never gave any other explanation?"

"No, the matter was dismissed as though it was unimportant."

"Well, Dr. Huxford," said Colonel Winthrop, stroking

his Vandyke, "what do you make of it?"

Huxford, bending his cane over his knee, smiled. "In that respect, Colonel, I'm inclined to agree with Dr. Hampden . . . My supposition at this time would be mere theory. However, some significant facts have been disclosed which I dare say may prove helpful."

"Do you believe this Dr. Schalkenbach is in New York?" Captain Sheldon asked.

"It's quite possible. I understand Colonel Winthrop's son Robert saw him at the opera."

The journalist frowned. "Then you mean to imply that the woman with him was young Winthrop's dead wife?"

Huxford paused, his eyes narrowed. "I should not care to comment on that at the moment," he replied. "There are several matters of greater importance to be looked into first."

"Don't you believe it is a case of mistaken identity?" persisted Hopewell.

Colonel Winthrop leaned forward with a stern look.

"Robert was certain about it," he said with emphasis.

"We must accept Robert's statement until we've satisfied ourselves as to the truth," put in Huxford. "Without an accepted premise as a basis, we could hardly argue."

"Of course, you know," added the journalist, turning to the criminologist, "it's an established psychological fact that a stranger is quite frequently mistaken for someone else a man or woman once loved. Even at the barest suggestion of anything once associated with the subject."

"I'm quite aware of all that," replied Huxford coolly.

"Well," and Hopewell shrugged, "I still must pooh-pooh the preposterous implication. Why, the only person, I understand, whoever rose from the dead was the Carpenter of Nazareth," he added caustically.

Huxford smiled faintly. "There are any number of authentic cases of suspended animation recorded in the annals of medical science," he remarked.

Captain Sheldon leaned forward. "I can vouch for a case which occurred when I was a boy," he said, knocking the ashes out of his pipe. "It was the death of a neighbor, Annie Falcon. And I attended her funeral with my parents. Three days before, she had been seized by a heart attack. She died the same day. There had been no previous symptons of the disease. The funeral rites and the astounding event which followed made quite an impression on my young mind.

"Annie had been a robust person, with a jolly disposition. In the village, where sensation is rare and marriages and funerals are the only exciting events, the sudden death of the cheerful Annie Falcon caused much grief, and almost the entire population turned out for her funeral. Six stalwart pallbearers carried her coffin into the cemetery chapel. To the solemn knell of the church bell, a procession of black-veiled mourners slowly followed. According to the custom there, the lid of the coffin was open, and the white face and sheeted body of the corpse was visible. The minister in his white robe stood before the casket. He was saying the last prayers when one of the pallbearers, eyes bulging in terror, turned and excitedly cried out, 'Look, Annie

Falcon is alive!' The mourners were utterly astonished. A hushed chatter swept the crowded chapel. The pallbearer had observed a scarcely perceptible amount of perspiration about the lips of the corpse.

"A physician was hastily summoned from among the mourners. Quickly he bled her wrist. The 'dead' Annie Falcon sat up in her coffin and looked about. Everybody stared as if hypnotized. Faint from days of starving and her horrifying experience, Annie uttered a gasping scream and fell back into her coffin, frightening some of the women mourners, who ran out of the chapel screaming hysterically."

Captain Sheldon paused. He lit his pipe. "The most dreadful part of the affair," he added, blowing a cloud of smoke, "was that Anne Falcon in her deathlike state, too weak to utter a whisper, could both see and hear, and later described the appalling experience of attending her own funeral."

"An excellent instance," acknowledged the Colonel. He turned to Huxford. "When you were in India, did you have an opportunity to witness the burying alive of a Yogi? Of course, the act of suspended animation is a power long claimed by the Hindus."

"Yes," replied Huxford. "The state the Yogi attains is called *samadai*. Although there are many reliable records of such burials, I was nevertheless curious about the phenomenon. I had the good fortune to be invited, with a group of other scientists, to witness one. A Yogi had attained *samadai*. He was buried deep in the ground. After forty days, he was dug up and we examined him. He was breathing very slightly.

"In order to accomplish the feat, the Yogi fell into a trance. His assistants stopped his nose, mouth, ears, and eyes with wax. The pulsation of the heart was so slight that I could scarcely detect it. I'm sure an unsuspecting medical examiner would have pronounced the Yogi dead. Then, wrapping him in a winding cloth, they lowered him into a grave and filled it with earth. A guard was placed about the spot day and night to prevent trickery. When the Yogi was uncovered forty days later, he was slightly emaciated but otherwise was little the worse for his remarkable experience."

The journalist reached over and poured himself a whisky. "I grant you," he said, holding up the glass in his hand, "there have been many cases of suspended animation, but today it would take more than a Rip VanWinkle or a Yogi to survive the undertaker." He gulped his drink and turned to the Colonel. "Surely Cynthia Winthrop was embalmed?"

"Of course!" the Colonel replied.

"May I inquire by whom?" Huxford asked.

The Colonel looked up sharply, "Conte & Marcus," he replied. "I'm sure there is no question about them."

"I may find it necessary to see them," Huxford remarked dryly.

"You don't expect foul play?" inquired Hopewell.

"On the contrary," replied Huxford coolly, "I know them to be reputable morticians. Among the most prominent in New York."

"You mean funeral engineers," the journalist prompted with a chuckle. "Why, that old glorified buzzard Marcus is the biggest hypocrite in the business. I knew him when he was a common corpse-snatcher. They used to tell the cubs on the old Herald, 'Find Marcus and you'll find the body."

The Colonel turned and motioned to the Negro attendant, who had been standing by taking in every word.

"Zipp, fetch us another bottle of seltzer," he ordered.

"Yessir, Colonel, yessir," said the Negro, grinning broadly. "Right away, yessir, Colonel," he added, bending over to pick up the tray.

"Oh, just a moment, Zipp," the Colonel said, taking hold of his arm and winking slyly at Huxford. "Here's a boy you can trust if you should have a graveyard job. He was my ace porter in the Congo."

The Negro straightened. "Yessir, Cap'n, Colonel, mister—in Africa, but not in the graveyard. Nossir, I doan' know nothin' about white folks risin' from the grave," he drawled, backing gingerly away, his flashing white eyes rolling. "Nossir, Cap'n, Colonel, mister, I sure doan', nossir."

Huxford smiled. "That's no joke, Zipp. I might need a good man."

"Yessir, mister, but I sure doan' know nothin'."

"That's just the sort of fellow I want," retorted Huxford.

"See nothing, hear nothing, and say nothing."

"Yessir, that's me—yessir," Zipp replied, shaking his head and grinning.

The journalist looked across to Colonel Winthrop. "If your son is so positive that he saw his wife with this Dr. Schalkenbach," he said, his leg hooked over the chair, swinging impatiently, "why not try to locate him?" He smiled cynically. "Surely a towering baboon shouldn't be hard to trap."

"Robert has bent every effort to locate him," the Colonel replied soberly.

Huxford frowned. "I trust he has not informed the police?" he said, holding his cane motionless.

"No, but that's an angle I've been worried about," the Colonel answered with some concern. "I shouldn't want this matter to become public."

"Don't be alarmed. The police would only laugh at such a fabulous tale," put in Hopewell.

Huxford twirled his cane. "What we've discussed I trust will remain confidential," he said, his tone serious.

"By no means must the press or the police learn of my interest in the affair. At, least for the present. Our ends will be served best if we work quietly."

The missionary's black eyes lighted. "Then, Professor Huxford, you're going to undertake the case?" he asked.

The criminologist nodded, his eyes narrowed. I'll cable immediately for a full report on Dr. Schalkenbach in Düsseldorf. I can do this through a friend connected with the German Gestapo, their Secret Police."

"And when would it be convenient for you to see

Robert?" the Colonel asked anxiously.

"If it can be arranged, I'd like to see him tomorrow. I understand he's resting at your place in Larchmont."

The Colonel nodded. "You know what this confounded blizzard has done to the roads—well, you had better come early and stay for dinner. I'd like you to see my collection of African trophies.

"Very well, I'll take an afternoon train."

6

THE express came to a grinding stop at the swank suburban town as a sumptuous black limousine swung up to the snow-blanketed platform. Sitting erect in the cushioned *tonneau*, his Vandyke beard suggesting the dignity of a British monarch, was Colonel Hadlow Winthrop. Rex Huxford stepped off the train, swinging his Malacca cane, and strode over to the car. A chauffeur in a raccoon coat opened the car door.

"I hardly expected your train to be on time," said the Colonel in greeting. "We had a record snowfall last night."

"The train was right on the dot," Huxford declared, glancing at his watch.

"I'm glad you are here this afternoon," the Colonel said, as the machine sped swishing over the packed snow. "Dr. Judd, our family physician, is expected. He has been attending Robert."

Huxford nodded. "And how is he today?"

"Much better. I told him you were going to take an active interest in the case. He is eager to talk with you."

"Does Dr. Judd know of the circumstances that brought about his condition?"

"Yes, Robert blurted the whole thing out to him. He seemed to find relief in telling it."

"Of course," said Huxford offhandedly. "I'm sure we can depend upon Dr. Judd's discretion?"

"Absolutely!" the Colonel replied. "One's family physician is often entrusted with the key to the closet that hides the family skeleton."

"What does he think of Robert's story?"

"He says it's preposterous—scoffed at it. I feel Robert was affronted by his attitude. It was Dr. Judd, of course, who attended Cynthia during her last illness."

"He did!"

"Yes, it was he who signed the death certificate."

Huxford's eyes narrowed. He fumbled with his cane and looked out at the passing landscape of hanging ice crystals and snow-mantled trees. "Does Dr. Judd live near you?" he asked absently.

"No. He lives in the village. He is consulting physician for the local hospital."

"I presume, then, that Robert and Cynthia were living here at your estate when she died?"

The Colonel slowly nodded. "After the loss of my wife I've found them a great comfort. Here we are now!" he added, as the car swept between two towering gateposts.

The long driveway passed through an archway of oaks and elms, now barren, and circled the rear of the house.

The Winthrop mansion, a rambling gray-stone structure of gabled and high-vaulted roofs, bay windows with pointed tops, balconies with balustrades, was high-lighted in the late winter sun. From the Gothic entrance, the trees surrounding the house spread their ice-laden branches skyward in fantastic patterns which stood out sharply against the somber dwelling. Isolated from the mainland on a narrow peninsula, the Gothic structure commanded an unobstructed view of the rocky shore line and Long Island Sound.

In the heavy oak-paneled drawing-room Colonel Winthrop and Rex Huxford stood before a lofty bay window.

"Quite a picture!" exclaimed Huxford, looking out on a panoramic view of the Sound, and across at the undulating hills of the North Shore of Long Island.

"In the distance is Huckleberry Island," pointed out the Colonel. "And to the south of the island is Execution Light."

"What a cheerful name for a lighthouse!" Huxford remarked.

"There is some significance attached to the name," the Colonel explained. "In Revolutionary times, before the light was built, British men-of-war were said to have sailed in close enough to the barren pile of rocks to put over a jollyboat of rebel malefactors. They were hanged and their bodies left dangling on gibbets to rot."

"A pleasant reminder of civilization!" commented

Huxford.

A massive carved oak door swung open. The Colonel and Huxford turned from the window. A pale-faced young man of medium height, in a well-tailored dark blue suit, entered.

"Dr. Huxford, this is my son Robert," Colonel Winthrop said.

Robert nodded, offering a cigarette and taking one himself.

His lips twitched a little.

"I'm still a bit unsteady," he said apologetically, slumping down on the arm of a lounge chair and drawing deep on his cigarette.

They drew up chairs. The criminologist noted the peculiar dryness of Robert's skin and the odd light-effect in his deep-set eyes; he particularly observed the pupils, which seemed to be abnormally dilated.

"The very thought of this thing terrifies me," Robert went on. "It has preyed on my mind until sleep is almost impossible. Dr. Judd has prescribed a sedative, but when I wake the ghastly thing confronts me again. You know how I loved Cynthia, Dad, and the terrible thought that Schalkenbach—" He rose quickly to his feet; his glassy-gray eyes lit wildly, his pale face turned chalk-white. "Good Lord!" he challenged, looking into Huxford's face, "Did you ever love a woman . . . put your trust . . . have your whole life and soul wrapped up in her . . . then, be cheated? . . . In the thought of her death" —he lowered his tone— "there is a certain peaceful satisfaction, a finality, a sort of sacred cloak which seals a love forever. But the horrible thought of Cynthia with this monster Schalkenbach . . . Yet that creature I saw with him is not, cannot be, my Cynthia! Don't you see?" he implored, raising his voice. "Something's got to be done. I simply can't go on."

"I understand." Huxford nodded sympathetically. "But you must first tell me what you have done to confirm your suspicions."

"Robert, tell Dr. Huxford what you found out at the box office of the Metropolitan," the Colonel urged.

More composed, Robert rested again on the arm of his chair. Drawing a neatly folded handkerchief from his breast pocket, he wiped the cold beads of perspiration from his forehead.

"You know" —he spoke slowly, lighting another cigarette— "it happened at the opera. Katherine Van Allen was with me, and our seats were in the orchestra at the left—in M, I remember. It was Monday night, and you know what the house is like then. You don't try to pick out any of your friends or acquaintances unless you know where they are sitting.

"The conductor raised his baton, and the usual hush fell over the audience. The overture to *Die Meistersinger* began. I had been looking around idly, but suddenly my attention was caught by a bulky figure in a grand-tier box on the right, near the front of the Horseshoe. I recognized Dr. Schalkenbach instantly. You could not mistake him."

Robert paused. His glassy eyes looked around the room and returned to Huxford. He gasped. "And then, I saw sitting at his side—Cynthia. I sat as if frozen. Could it be an illusion? I looked again. My heart beat fast. I felt faint. Beyond the shadow of a doubt it was Cynthia—but what a ghostly, strange Cynthia."

"Did Miss Van Allen also see them?" interrupted Huxford.

"No," he answered, "I am sure Katherine did not notice them."

"And she does not know?" asked Huxford quizzically. Robert shook his head.

"No," he faltered, "I . . . I didn't dare to mention it to her. She has been very close to me, and to tell her that . . ."

Colonel Winthrop raised his eyebrows. He shifted his steel-gray eyes to his son.

"Katherine is broad-minded," he said reassuringly. "I'm sure she would understand."

Robert turned restlessly on the arm of the chair. "It was an incongruous picture," he continued, pausing long enough to smudge out his cigarette and light another. "Schalkenbach's bulk protruding over the box was like a grimacing gargoyle. Cynthia, her slender body in rich black, her clean-cut pallid face and radiant black eyes staring as if she were a sleepwalker, was like a fragile classic statue beside this grotesque monster. With his thick lips, bulging ungainly in his evening dress and stiff shirt, he suggested a travesty on civilized man."

"A case of Beauty and the Beast," remarked Huxford dryly.

"Yes," nodded Robert between puffs of smoke. It was

an extraordinary sight to see his powerful figure swinging in unison with the rumbling Wagnerian music. As the scores of violins and brasses sounded in the bass, rising tumultuously to a dazzling climax, kettledrums thundering the assertive theme of the pompous opera, Schalkenbach clenched his massive hands as if he felt that he himself was the great *Meistersinger*.

"When the lights went up after the first act, Schalkenbach and Cynthia had disappeared. Without saying anything to Katherine, I looked for them when we went out into the foyer, but there was no sign of them. They reappeared in the box shortly after the second act had begun. And during the next intermission they disappeared in exactly the same way. I was handicapped by Katherine's presence—I couldn't leave her. Their disappearance puzzled me—they must have gone into the private dressing-room in the rear of the box. Of course, I thought I could trace them later."

Robert paused, took a few puffs. "When the curtain was drawn on the last act, Cynthia rose. Towering above her, Schalkenbach spread her black cape. The rich lining flashed scarlet as he swung it about her porcelain-white loveliness. I still hoped to encounter them in the foyer, but it was almost impossible to make our way through the slowly moving throng. They must have left by a side exit, for I did not see them again."

"Then what did you learn at the box office?" Huxford asked.

"I made inquiry there early the next day. At first, the

man at the office was reluctant to give me any in. formation. When I presented my card, however, he became friendlier. After thumbing some pages of a ledger, he told me that the occupants of the box were listed as Baron and Baroness Renfels van Amste! No address was given."

"Wasn't that a bit irregular?" Huxford questioned.

"Yes, I thought so myself," replied Robert. "But when I asked the man about it he smiled rather superciliously. 'Of course, you know, Mr. Winthrop,' he exclaimed with a gesture, 'that the Metropolitan's policy is to extend every courtesy to its patrons.'

"'Then you must know Baron van Amstel?' I asked politely, trying not to give myself away.

"The man frowned. 'I'm afraid, Mr. Winthrop,' he answered, 'that's a little slip-up. Frankly, I never heard of this Baron van Amste!' You see, it was an advance cash transaction at the window. The reservation, according to the ledger, was made by telephone.'"

"Apparently," Huxford remarked, "Dr. Schalkenbach is sailing under false colors."

"That's just, what puzzles me," agreed Robert, his eyes brightening. If everything were aboveboard, why would he be posing as a baron? There's something wrong somewhere."

Colonel Winthrop spoke up. "I don't doubt it. But you know what an attraction a European title is in New York."

"Yes," agreed Robert impatiently, "I grant you that, Dad . . . but if it were just the case of a bogus nobleman trying to crash society, there would be some ostentation, some ballyhoo. In this instance, we can't even locate the man."

"Is that as far as you have gone?" Huxford asked.

A look of dismay crossed Robert's face. "Yes." He nodded, "I've had private detectives search for listings under Amstel and Schalkenbach. The agency reported that not a trace of either could be found in the city. I'm afraid we are up a blind alley."

Huxford's eyes narrowed.

"I think it the better part of discretion to keep this affair strictly private," he advised sternly. "My connection with the investigation should under no circumstances be mentioned. Please understand, I think it best that when Dr. Judd comes I'm merely the guest of your father."

Robert nodded in assent.

"It's just as well the old fossil be kept in the dark," he said more cheerfully. "He laughed at me when I told him my story."

"You can hardly blame him," put in Colonel Winthrop. "Your insinuation that Cynthia may not be dead offends his professional dignity."

"He's just an artful chest-thumper," retorted Robert. "A family fixture, no more than a retainer. For every ailment he has a different colored pill. I can't see why we tolerate him "

"You're a bit unstrung," interrupted the Colonel coolly. "Your remarks are hasty, and I am sure unjustified. Dr. Judd is a competent physician. When you were a child and down with typhoid it was he who pulled you through."

"Yes," agreed Robert with a cynical smile, "that's the one big feather in his cap. But Mother . . . and Cynthia?"

Colonel Winthrop's gray eyes turned almost black in somber intensity as he stared reproachfully at Robert.

His lips moved slightly as if he were going to speak.

After an awkward silence Huxford turned to Robert.

"What kind of a pill has Dr. Judd prescribed this time?" he asked blandly.

"Little white tablets of morphine."

"A rather strong narcotic," Huxford remarked, glancing speculatively at Robert, and reflecting how many times be had observed the same telltale marks in others. He wondered, noting the young man's sallow face and dark-circled eyes, how far he had gone in the use of morphine. He knew what fabulous exaggerations and lies a user of narcotics was capable of. Could Robert's whole story be a fantasy induced by the drug? Or was there behind it something more sinister? Confronting Robert, he demanded:

"How long has this use of morphine been going on?"

Robert's face broke into a strained smile, "Why," he said as though dismissing the subject, "it's only been a few days—I couldn't sleep."

A butler in a swallow-tailed coat and striped trousers entered the room.

"Dr. Judd is here, sir," the butler announced, standing stiffly.

The physician, a wizened, gray-haired man carrying a small black bag, his lanky legs striding loosely, entered.

His beady eyes swept the group curiously.

"Just dropped in for a moment," he said in a slightly nasal tone. "I hope I'm not intruding?"

"Not in the least," Colonel Winthrop responded warmly, rising to greet him. "Dr. Judd, I'd like you to meet my old friend Dr. Rex Huxford."

The physician's piercing black eyes snapped. "So, you're the famous criminologist!" he said in some surprise, shaking hands. "I followed the Whalen case, and was particularly interested in your autopsy work on rare poisons. I'm honored to meet you."

Huxford smiled deprecatingly. "I'm afraid the papers were a bit sensational," he replied.

Colonel Winthrop stirred restlessly. "Dr. Huxford is also interested in zoology," he remarked. "He has come out to see my African collection."

A frown broke the wrinkles of Dr. Judd's face. "I'm sure you'll find the gorilla specimens the most interesting," he said, with a certain dryness that puzzled Huxford.

"My father," Robert spoke up, "is the only person ever to capture a female gorilla and bring her back alive."

"Yes," acknowledged the Colonel, "I named her Miss Congo, but after a year in captivity she died." He paused reflectively. "I'll never forget the feeling that came over me when I captured her," he said sadly. "I had to shoot her mate, a massive gorilla that stood up and stretched his long arms high over his manlike head. He was pathetically human as he towered balancing on his short legs, gazing benignly at me. Suddenly he charged. On he came, like a man with his hands upraised in submission. I held off as long as I dared, but I had to shoot. The old bugger dropped. I felt as if I had taken a human life."

Dr. Judd's black eyes searched the room and returned to Colonel Winthrop.

"Your gorilla tale," he said with slight emphasis, his irregular teeth showing as he grinned, "suggests Robert's good friend Schalkenbach. I suppose," he added, turning his furrowed face and fixing his eyes quizzically on Huxford, "Robert has told you about him?"

Robert looked up sharply. A flush of resentment lighted the paleness of his face. His lips moved as if it were difficult to hold himself back. He drew a cigarette and mechanically tapped it on his wrist.

"Yes." Huxford nodded calmly. "He did speak of him. Are you acquainted with the man?"

"No!" the physician replied sharply. "But I understand he's quite a miracle-worker in the medical arts and," he went on somewhat caustically, "a devotee of the opera." Turning to Robert, he said more amiably, "I see there's nothing I can do for you." Reaching for his bag, he looked up, his shriveled face breaking into a grin. "I must go," he said curtly. His beady eyes glinting, he turned and abruptly walked away.

A stillness fell over the oak-paneled room as the heavy door shut on the gaunt figure of Dr. Judd. Huxford, his eyes almost closed, fingered the buttonhole of his lapel. He turned to Colonel Winthrop and Robert, who were waiting for him to break the silence.

"This is indeed an extraordinary situation," he declared. "It suggests the case of a vampire—"

"You can't mean that!" gasped Robert.

"One never knows," replied Huxford offhandedly.

"'There are more things in heaven and earth, Horatio, than are dreamt of in your philosophy.' In spite of the number of unfounded superstitions, there are numerous cases of vampires recorded from reliable sources."

"The superstition," put in Colonel Winthrop soberly, "is still quite prevalent in parts of eastern Europe. When I was in Port Said en route to Mombasa I heard at first hand of a case. I have no reason to doubt the authenticity of the story. It was told to me by an eyewitness, an English gentleman of high rank. But when you bring it to my own door . . . I admit I'm skeptical."

"Just what do you mean when you say vampire?" demanded Robert.

A smile played about the corners of Huxford's mouth. "According to the Encyclopaedia Britannica," he said dryly, "a vampire is a bloodsucking ghost or reanimated body of a dead person—the soul of a person believed to come from the grave and wander about sucking the blood of persons who are asleep, causing their death. Those who turn vampires are generally wizards, suicides, those who come to a violent end, or those who have been cursed by their parents or by the Church. A living dead body!" Huxford smiled. "The words are idle, contradictory, incomprehensible—but so are vampires."

Robert leaned tensely forward.

"Do you know of any actual cases?" he asked.

"Indeed," replied Huxford, "there are many examples to be found among the folk tales of the Slavonic peoples. One is found in the *Lettres Jérives*.

"In the beginning of one September," he continued slowly, "there died in the village of Kisibova, some distance from Graditz, an old man who was sixty-two years of age. Three days after he had been buried, he appeared in the night to his son and asked him for something to eat. The son having given him something, he ate and disappeared. The next day the son recounted to his neighbors what had happened. That night the father did not appear, but the following night he showed himself and again asked for something to eat. The neighbors did not know whether the son gave him anything or not, but the next day after that the son was found dead in his bed. On the same day, five or six persons fell suddenly ill in the village, and in a few days they died one after the other.

"The bailiff of the place, when informed of what had happened, sent an account of it to the tribunal of Belgrade, which dispatched to the village two officers to examine into the affair, and an executioner. The imperial officers, from whom we have this account, went there from Graditz to find out what they could.

"The officials opened the graves of those who had been dead six weeks. When they came to that of the old man, they found him with his eyes open, having fine color, with natural respiration, nevertheless motionless as the dead. From this they concluded that he was undoubtedly a vampire. The executioner drove a stake into his heart, then they raised a pyre and reduced the corpse to ashes. No marks of vampirism were found on any of the other corpses."

Huxford relaxed, drew a cigarette, and lit it.

"A story which I think will better illustrate my point," he went on, "is the Russian tale told by Madame Blavatsky in *Isis Unveiled*. She states that she had the account from an eye-witness of the occurrence.

"Before the Revolution—" he paused, settled back in his chair and blew a ring of smoke—" there occurred in Russia one of the most frightful cases of vampirism on record. The governor of Kamien was a man of about sixty years who was of a cruel and jealous disposition. Clothed with despotic authority, he exercised it ruthlessly as his brutal instincts prompted. He fell in love with the pretty daughter of a subordinate officer. Although the girl was betrothed to a young man whom she loved, the tyrant forced her father to give her to him in marriage, and the poor victim, despite her despair, became his wife. His jealous disposition soon exhibited itself. He beat her, confined her to her room for weeks together, and prevented her seeing anyone except in his presence. Finally, he fell sick and died. When he found his end approaching, he made her swear never to marry again, and with fearful oaths threatened that in case she did so he would return from his grave and kill her. He was buried in the cemetery across the river, and the young widow experienced no further annoyance until, gelling the better of her fears, she listened to the importunities of her former lover, and they were again betrothed.

"On the night of the customary betrothal feast, when all in the house had gone to bed, the old mansion was aroused by shrieks proceeding from her room. The doors were burst open, and the unhappy woman was found lying on her bed in a swoon. At the same time, a carriage was heard rumbling out of the courtyard. Her body was black and blue in places, as from the effects of pinches, and from a slight puncture in her neck drops of blood were oozing. Upon recovery from her faint, she stated that her deceased husband had suddenly entered her room, appearing exactly as in life with the exception of a dreadful pallor; that he had upbraided her for her inconstancy, and then beaten and pinched her most cruelly. Her story was disbelieved, but the next morning the guard stationed at the other end of the bridge which spans the river reported that just before midnight a black coach-and-six had driven furiously past without answering their challenge.

"The new governor, who disbelieved the story of the apparition, nevertheless took the precaution of doubling the guards across the bridge. The same thing happened, however, night after night. The soldiers declared that the toll bar at their station near the bridge would rise of itself, and the spectral equipage would sweep past them despite their efforts to stop it. At the same time every night the watchers, including the widow's family and the servants, were thrown into a heavy sleep. And every morning the young victim was found bruised, bleeding, and in a swoon as before. The town was thrown into consternation. The physicians had no explanation to offer. Priests came to pass the night in prayer, but as midnight approached, all were seized with the same terrible lethargy. Finally, the archbishop of the province came and performed the ceremony of exorcism in person. On the following morning, the governor s widow was found worse than ever. She had now been brought to death's door.

"The new governor was finally driven to take the severest measures to stop the ever-increasing panic in the town. He stationed fifty Cossacks along the bridge, with orders to stop the spectral carriage at all hazards. Promptly at the usual hour it was heard and seen approaching from the direction of the cemetery. The officer of the guard and a priest bearing a crucifix planted themselves in front of the toll bar and together shouted, 'In the name of God and the Czar, who goes there?' Out of the coach was thrust a well-remembered head, and a familiar voice responded, 'The Privy Councilor of State and Governor Konin!' At the same moment the officer, the priest, and the soldiers were flung aside, as by an electric shock, and the ghostly equipage passed them before they could recover breath.

"The archbishop then resolved as a last expedient to resort to the time-honored plan of exhuming the body and driving an oaken stake through the heart. This was done with great religious ceremony in the presence of the whole populace. The story is that the body was found gorged with blood, and with red cheeks and lips. At the instant that the first blow was struck upon the stake a groan issued from the corpse and a jet of blood spouted high into the air. The archbishop pronounced the usual exorcism, the body was reinterred, and from that time no more was heard of the vampire."

Pale, Robert turned to Huxford. "Surely you don't think Cynthia has become this terrible thing?" he asked incredulously.

"The whole affair is so extraordinary," Huxford replied quietly, bending forward to smudge out his cigarette in an ash tray, "that I shouldn't care to venture a definite opinion at the moment."

"I have very little faith in that point of view," commented Colonel Winthrop. "Perhaps, Dr. Huxford, you have formulated some more substantial basis on which to go ahead?"

"I have," he replied quickly. "I've given the problem serious consideration. There are a number of possible solutions to this case. I have formulated three separate and distinct hypotheses. One holds, I believe, the key to this case.

"What I'm about to propose is the initial step in proving the truth or falsity of this hypothesis. Everything we might do before taking this step is merely rationalizing. And if we do not act on what I propose it will be futile to proceed further. What I wish to do will require the services of three men who can be trusted and who can also be depended upon to hold their tongues. I know of two such men. I once helped them during Prohibition when they were in a tight spot. I'm sure they would jump at the chance if they saw some cash in it. For the third, I might suggest the Negro attendant at the Explorers Club—your porter boy in Africa."

"Why, yes . . . yes. Yes, of course," said the Colonel, nodding.

"Does the same dentist attend all the members of your family?"

The Colonel looked a little puzzled, then nodded.

"Yes, Dr. Zell has done our dental work for years."

"He did Cynthia's?"

"Yes."

"I'd like him to help me in a matter of identification."

Robert turned quickly to Huxford. "What is it you propose?" he demanded.

"I want to exhume the body of Cynthia Winthrop, and since to avoid publicity is most important, to do it privately."

The Colonel abruptly rose.

"Of course," he said in a cold but excited tone, "we want to help you, but isn't that a rather drastic step? And isn't it illegal?"

The criminologist narrowed his eyes at the Colonel. "Yes, it is. But under the circumstances I consider that we are justified in breaking that particular law. If we ask for permission there will be publicity, and this is a case where we must avoid it." He paused, then said in a tone of quiet finality "The exhumation is essential. Without it, further steps would be fruitless."

7

AN awesome silence hung over the cemetary. Tombstones spread like upright dominoes in an endless line over the slopes of the snow-mantled graves. Ice crystals hung in the air. Out of the darkness of the night crept the black outline of a limousine. Slowly it rolled to a creaking stop alongside the high wall of the cemetery.

In the car were the figures of five men. Those in the *tonneau* leaned stiffly forward. Their Fedora hats, which almost hid their burly faces, were dimly shadowed against the frosted windows. One pressed his pudgy nose against the clouded glass; he peered out wild-eyed, his swarthy face a sickly green in the yellow moonlight.

In the driver's seat sat Rex Huxford, his Malacca cane hanging lightly on his arm. Alongside the criminologist snuggled a dumpy figure, hunched over as though trying to keep out the bitter cold. Huxford glanced at the clock on the dash. It showed ten minutes past midnight.

He looked ahead. The snow-furrowed road ran on for some distance, then curved abruptly up a hill around the cemetery. It seemed to be deserted.

"Dr. Zell," he said in a low voice to the man beside him, "you stay with me. "Turning, he reached over his shoulder and slid open the glass window back of the driver's seat. "All right, boys—snap into it," he ordered through the aperture. "When you've dug up the casket, bring it to us. We'll be waiting inside the Winthrop mausoleum. Spike bas the layout."

"O. K., Boss," muttered a stocky fellow. "Leave the works to us."

Spike Salieno and big pug-faced partner, Plugger Martin, clambered out of the car. Zipp, fumbling with shovel, pickax, and a coil of rope, reluctantly followed.

The car moved on into the darkness.

"Come on, black boy," Plugger Martin ordered between his teeth, "get the hell over that wall!"

Zipp's eyes showed white.

"I never knowed white folks wanted me go prowlin' round graveyards," he whined, shuffling along behind the two plug-uglies. "I sure ain't for foolin' around them dead folks."

The two men pulled themselves up on the wall. They reached down to give Zipp a lift. "Say, nigger, shove me yuh mit," demanded Spike as they dragged his dead weight over the high stone fence. "You're comin' along and like it."

"That's all right, Mr. Spike," the Negro drawled, struggling with the coil of rope. "I'se goin'."

Spike Salieno led the way, breaking the crusted snow. Plugger Martin, laden with implements, followed in his footprints, while Zipp floundered along close behind. They trudged on in silence over crypts and past vaults, to the accompaniment of crunching snow.

Plugger stumbled and fell forward, the implements scattering in the snow. He got up and spat in disgust, a quid of tobacco landing on a tombstone. Gathering the implements, he slung them over his shoulder, muttering in lurid blasphemy, "Bastard of a night to snatch a moll what's croaked!"

Spike cocked his head. "Say, pipe down on tha squawkin'," he bawled. "What yuh beefin' about? You're gettin' yuh cut, ain't yuh?"

The moon moved behind a low overhanging cloud that seemed to hover over the graveyard. The stubby shadows of tombstones and the weird outlines of images vanished. The men groped on in the blackness and biting cold.

Spike stopped short. The others halted in their tracks. They stood stiffly, like black statues frozen to the ground. Whipping out a flashlight, Spike swept its beam hesitantly from tombstone to tombstone. A large white cross brightened in its yellow path. As though in reverence, he held the light on it. Plugger gaped, and involuntarily crossed himself. Spike swung the beam away. The spotlight swept the seraphic statue of an angel with its hands out in supplication. He played the beam over it. At the base of the monument it caught the dark leaves of a wreath. Slipping the flashlight back in his pocket, he cocked his head over his shoulder, he ordered: "Come on, mugs, here's tha grave."

Spike stepped forward and picked up the wreath.

"That's the finger what tha boss puts in today," he mumbled, ringing it over the head of the angel. Then throwing off his coat, he grabbed a pick, spat on each hand, and brought the implement down with force into the ground.

Plugger bent over his spade. Zipp crouched at the foot of the grave. The somber figures of the three men bobbing beneath the guardian angel looking on in mute acquiescence, its hands extended out over them as though in supplication, made a strange picture.

~§~

In accordance with the plan Huxford and Spike Salieno had worked out in the afternoon, Huxford parked the limousine off the main road. He and the dentist climbed the wall and silently made their way through the unbroken snow toward the Winthrop mausoleum. The moon broke through the black hovering clouds. Huxford looked up. Above on the sloping ground projected a stone tomb. In the soft moonlight its white bulk stood out on the bleak hillside, a huge marble cubicle.

They stepped up to the mausoleum's low entrance. The steady thud of digging sounded distantly.

"The boys are hard at it," Huxford remarked under his breath, taking from his pocket a large key. He fumbled with a chain and opened the gate. Jiggling the key in the lock, he slowly pushed the creaking iron door inward. Distorted shadows of the gate bars fell across the floor and walls. A warm musty odor greeted them as they groped their way into the vault.

Huxford flicked on his flashlight. The figures of the criminologist in his trim, bell-shaped overcoat and the squatty dentist in his turned-down hat and upturned collar paused in the doorway of the tomb. Huxford played the light about the chamber. Projecting above the marble floor, side by side, were two oblong sepulchers. Huxford snapped off his light. The pallid moonlight streamed into the vault. They sat down on the stone slabs of a sepulcher.

~§~

At the grave, the mound of loose dirt was steadily rising as the two men, their heads almost out of sight, heaved up the earth.

A rustling noise like the fluttering swish of a covey of birds taking sudden flight sounded from back of the grave. Startled, Zipp saw the enormous shadow of out-stretched wings on the snow. His eyes bulged white in the darkness; he dropped the coil of rope he was holding.

A strong beam of light in the distance slowly swung through the cemetery. Plugger Martin's head popped up above the piled earth.

"Duck, nigger!" he shouted.

Zipp sprawled prostrate on the snow. The light swept through the graveyard and vanished. The tense stillness was broken by a long forlorn: *"Whooooooooooo!"* The eerie sound continued, *"Whooooooooooo!"* The Negro thrust his head into the snow, burying it like an ostrich. The earth under him moved. His body grew rigid; his teeth chattered. He felt as though a cold, clammy hand was pressing against his stomach and moving slowly toward his throat.

The ground bulged under him again. His hat rose on his head.

"Lord save me!" he cried out in terror. "It comin' outa de grave!"

The two plug-uglies jerked themselves up out of the excavation, leaped over the piled earth. A large owl fluttered away from a near-by tree.

"What's eatin' yuh?" gruffly demanded Plugger.

Shaking, his eyes popping, Zipp pointed speechlessly at the heaving ground. Shoving him to one side, Plugger shot his spade into the ground in front of the moving mound. With a grin he unearthed a mole, which scurried away like a wharf rat.

"Say, yuh mugs," Spike barked, "cut tha comedy. Get goin'!"

Picking up the rope, Plugger jumped back into the open grave. He looped it around the ends of the encrusted box and crawled out over the loose earth. Hand over hand Plugger and Zipp laboriously raised the box containing a metal coffin. Zipp slackened his effort, the casket tilted.

"Hey! Steady, youse guys," cautioned Spike, watching. "What the hell yuh think this is—?"

"Yessir, yessir," the Negro grunted. "Yessir, Mr. Spike."

They worked the casket out of the hole and dragged it over the loose earth. Plugger held the flashlight while Spike unscrewed the heavy screws of the outer box, lifted off the wooden lid, and extracted the casket, leaving the box by the grave. Grasping the coffin by its thick handles, the two plug-uglies in front, Zipp struggling with the back, they wobbled down the slope toward the mausoleum.

A shadow darkened the entrance of the tomb. Huxford rose to his feet. The dismal, lumbering procession staggered into the chamber.

"Put it down here, boys," he directed, pointing with his cane to the stone-slabbed sepulcher on which they had been sitting. "And loosen the lid."

The Negro released his end and backed away toward the door, his eyes fixed upon the coffin. Spike slid the bolts of the metal lid. Huxford stepped up with his light. Gripping the hinged lid, he forced the lid up with a piercing creak. The sound echoed wierdly in the hollow tomb, it slowly opened, until it stood erect. He played the light on the white dress of the corpse.

Zipp cringed against the marble wall, his eyes bulging in their sockets. Without changing his sober expression, Spike took off his hat and bowed his head. He turned to Plugger, who was dumbly staring and biting into a plug of tobacco. "Doff your lid!" he ordered, jabbing him in the ribs with his elbow. "Ain't yuh got no respect for tha dead?" Plugger awkwardly removed his Fedora and solemnly crossed himself.

Huxford held the spotlight on the emaciated corpse, revealing its folded arms, its ghastly hollow cheeks and black sunken eyes.

"Hum!" he commented. "In quite a state of preservation."

He took hold of the arm of the flabby little dentist.

"Step up closer, Doctor," he requested. Then in a more formal tone, he added: "Dr. Zell, you were acquainted with the deceased Cynthia Winthrop, wife of Robert Winthrop, and did her dental work?"

"Yes . . . yes," Zell faltered, "that's true."

"Then you, Dr. Zell," he began, speaking rapidly, pointing with his cane at the figures watching gingerly in the background, their hats off and heads bowed, "a licensed practicing dentist of Larchmont, Westchester County, State of New York, are competent to judge the identity of the deceased in the presence of these witnesses."

"Yes," he gasped, "I am."

"Then you are sure of the identity of this woman?"

Dr. Zell fumbled in his pocket, took out a pair of glasses, and adjusted them to his nose. He cleared his throat. "Why, yes!" he declared. "That is Mrs. Winthrop."

Huxford narrowed the spotlight. "Examine her teeth," he ordered. The pudgy dentist bent down over the corpse. Pulling a pair of forceps from the bag he carried, he probed into the mouth of the cadaver.

"No, not that," the little man muttered half to himself, consulting a paper in his hand, "molar gold crown . . . no gold inlay . . . filling right upper . . ."

Suddenly he stiffened. He looked sheepishly.

"Why, this isn't her dental work!" he announced.

"You will note," he pointed out, astonished, as Huxford bent close with the light, "that this woman has conspicuous gold fillings. I would never think of putting such work in the mouth of any patient," he added with disdain.

The criminologist rose, his eyes almost shut.

"I take it, Dr. Zell," he said quietly, "that you are sure of your work?"

"Absolutely!"

"Then you are positive that this is not Cynthia Winthrop's body?"

"Positive!"

Huxford paused and straightened.

"Thank you," he said simply.

8

THE morning sun streamed through the Gothic bay window, bathing the dark drawingroom in a flood of warmth. Colonel Winthrop leaned stiffly forward in his chair. His face and voice betrayed strain.

"Good Lord . . . what you insinuate is horrible! You don't think . . . ?"

"That's not the question," Huxford coolly replied, settling back. "The very fact that the body is not Cynthia Winthrop's raises several perplexing problems. It's a delicate situation, and one that must—"

"But, my God," interrupted the Colonel, "what a fantastic, cunning, ingenious—"

"Undoubtedly," cut in Huxford, "it's a most extraordinary situation. And we are dealing with a crafty person whose subtle strategy may become an even greater menace."

"Incredible" muttered Colonel Winthrop. "I don't understand." He shook his head. "How could a substitution have possibly occurred? Why, we positively saw her body before it went to the undertaker. What on earth could have happened?"

"That I cannot answer at the moment, the criminologist replied. "There are a lot of loose ends which will have to be gathered and connected. You say young Mrs. Winthrop died of a strange malady which your family physician, Dr. Judd, thought was sleeping sickness?"

"Yes." The Colonel nodded gravely. "Before death took her, she lapsed into a deep sleep which lasted nine days. Dr. Judd can give you the details."

"Did Dr. Judd question you when told I wanted to see him?"

"No. Very little was said. He seemed perfectly willing."

"Well," said Huxford, "your son, at least, should be glad to learn of this. It will gratify him, I believe, to feel that credence is given his story. Even believing this ghastly thing is better than fearing that he is suffering from an insane illusion."

"Then you're convinced that Cynthia is alive?"

Huxford's eyes narrowed a little. "The facts that we have a death certificate and no corpse and that another body lies in her grave lead me to believe Cynthia Winthrop lives."

"Is it possible that her body could have been taken for

medical study?"

"No, hardly that. The exhumation disclosed an unidentified corpse. That is not the work of ghouls. Cadavers, these days, are legally furnished by our charitable institutions."

"It doesn't seem credible," the Colonel said, slowly shaking his head. "And you believe she disappeared between the time of her alleged death and the interment?"

"Yes," asserted Huxford. "Perhaps even before. Of course, unless there was some negligence on the part of the undertaker."

"Conte & Marcus are one of the oldest firms in New York. I'm confident they're beyond reproach, despite Hopewell's absurd remarks."

"I agree, but as a matter of routine I'll be obliged to look into the burial permit and learn if the body was embalmed by them."

"It's disgraceful—utterly disgraceful," Colonel Winthrop lamented. "Could it possibly be that she was influenced to become a party to this beastly affair?"

Huxford frowned. "I'm afraid," he said quietly, his eyes almost shut, "that our little problem can't be reduced to the simplicity of the usual 'triangle'. Our principal, in this case, is a fiend whose superior knowledge of biology, I fear, has involved him in an experiment beyond the realm of our present comprehension."

"Good God!" gasped Colonel Winthrop. "Surely you don't think . . . ?"

"Hello!" Robert said, walking briskly into the room,

fresh and immaculate. "I'm sorry," he apologized, shaking hands with Huxford, "I hardly expected you so early."

Then, tensely, "What happened last night?"

"Dr. Huxford discovered that Cynthia's body was not buried in her grave," said Colonel Winthrop soberly. "He found the corpse of an unknown woman."

The criminologist nodded. "I shall not concede your wife's death until we have found her body."

"I cannot be surprised under the circumstances," declared Robert. "I have some further news—I saw Cynthia last night!"

"What?" demanded Colonel Winthrop. "You don't mean you spoke to her?"

"No, I couldn't. But I had Kent Jaimson follow her. He's going to let me know this morning where she went and anything else he can learn."

"Quite a coincidence, your seeing her again," remarked Huxford dryly.

"No," contradicted Robert, "I don't think you'd call it exactly a coincidence, she was expecting me, I am sure. But I couldn't get away to speak to her. Katherine was with me this time too."

"Where was it?" Huxford questioned.

"On Sixty-Seventh Street near Central Park West. Katherine and Kent and I had just come out of the *Café des Artistes* when I saw a woman staring at me through the window of a taxicab. She must have been waiting for me outside, for when we walked up the street, her cab followed us in the jumble of traffic. It crept up to us. The woman beckoned. I thought she had mistaken me for someone else. Then light fell on her face and I recognized her at once. There was a pleading look about her black staring eyes that made me feel she was under some kind of restraint and needed help. Taking Kent by the arm, I drew him aside and asked him to follow her."

"How did Miss Van Allen take it?"

"Oh, Katherine!" he answered quickly, his eyes brightening. "She's a swell sport . . . she took it good-naturedly. When she saw Cynthia beckoning from the cab window she said, 'Does she want you, Robert? Who is she?' Nudging Kent, I spoke to him quietly. He took his cue at once. Excusing himself, he jumped into a taxi at the curb and disappeared. I hardly think Katherine suspected anything."

"Did Kent Jaimson realize the seriousness of his mission?"

"Yes, I think so. He's a close friend. I had told him everything. But I don't know whether he felt certain it was Cynthia."

"Jaimson and Robert were classmates at college," explained Colonel Winthrop. "He was an All-American football player."

Huxford nodded. "I recall now. He was the famous quarterback the newspapers played up a few years ago. No doubt he's the type of chap who can handle himself in almost any situation."

"You can leave it to him," assured Robert. He's the rough-and-ready sort, the kind who enjoys being in a tight spot. And now I feel it won't be long before we know the hiding-place of Schalkenbach. I'm sure Kent won't fail."

Huxford closed his eyes and rested his head on the back of his chair.

"It would seem that you are being watched," he said slowly. "I'm agreed with you that your meeting in front of the Café des Artistes was not just a coincidence. There's a hidden motive back of this, and I wouldn't be surprised to find that Dr. Schalkenbach isn't working alone."

A door opened. The three looked up, startled by the appearance of Dr. Judd. His tall gaunt figure was bending before them before the butler could announce his arrival. His presence met with a frigid silence. Clinging onto his little black satchel, he scowled down into their faces.

"I see we meet again," he said bitingly. "What's it this time—more zoology?"

Colonel Winthrop rose and faced the physician.

"Dr. Huxford," he said, "would like you to answer some questions concerning Cynthia's death."

The Doctor's beady eyes flashed.

"Nothing mysterious about it," he grunted. "The death certificate plainly stated the facts."

"I haven't seen the certificate," Huxford cut in casually. "I understand she was stricken by sleeping sickness. The type common to this continent, no doubt?"

"Why, yes . . . yes," he faltered. "Yes, of course— encephalitis lethargica."

"And she developed lethargy at the outset?" Huxford asked sharply.

A scowl cracked the physician's leathery, wizened face. He hesitated. His thin lips grew taut and his small black eyes glared.

"What is this, an inquisition?" he demanded fiercely, staring down at father and son. "Cynthia Winthrop," he replied vehemently, "is positively dead and six feet under!"

A strained silence followed the physician's outbreak. Robert lit a cigarette. Colonel Winthrop cleared his throat, swallowing heavily, and turned to the criminologist.

"Dr. Huxford," he said, slowly shaking his steel-gray head, "I believe you can best explain to Dr. Judd—there seems to be some misunderstanding."

"Yes," Huxford acknowledged. Then, turning to the physician, he nodded suavely. "Won't you sit down?"

Without shifting the narrowed gaze of his intense black eyes, the doctor, still holding onto his little black satchel, settled into a chair and raked his lanky legs up before him.

"Dr. Judd," Huxford said, looking him in the eye, "it may interest you to know . . . I've reason to believe that Cynthia Winthrop still lives."

"Preposterous!" scoffed the physician. "I won't believe it."

"It may interest you further to know," Huxford continued coolly, "that last night the body in her grave was exhumed. With the assistance of her dentist, Dr. Zell, we found that it was not the body of Cynthia Winthrop, but the cadaver of an unidentified woman."

"That's impossible!" Judd declared. "I saw her dead

with my own eyes—saw her and examined her. Do you think I write a death certificate without making sure what I am doing? Can you produce the corpse?"

"The body has been reburied. If necessary, Dr. Judd" —Huxford's tone became emphatic—" I shall request an official exhumation . . . I might find it necessary to demand an autopsy."

The physician scowled.

"Even if what you say is true, a rash move might precipitate a most embarrassing situation," he rejoined caustically. "I'm sure the Winthrops wouldn't relish the notoriety. An unaccounted-for corpse in the family is a thing not easily explained."

Huxford nodded.

"Yes, quite true," he answered sharply. "And especially embarrassing to the physician who signed the death certificate. Frankly, Dr. Judd," he added in a lower tone, "it's not my wish to call in the police. I hope to keep this a strictly private affair. I believe we can handle it without dragging the name of Winthrop into print. I fully sympathize with your point of view, Doctor. But what you have to tell me of her illness may be of importance."

The physician's eyes brightened.

"Very well," he said more affably, after a slight pause. "At first, I was a little uncertain about Mrs. Winthrop's illness. To be honest, I was puzzled by the symptoms that developed. There was an irregular fever which became hectic. Then she became somnolent, and on the fourth day lapsed into a deep sleep, from which she was never aroused."

"Were there any previous symptoms?"

"No, her health bad been excellent. She complained of neuralgic pains before lethargy developed."

"I understand a state of coma set in nine days before she succumbed. Were there symptoms of anemia?"

"Yes. And followed by considerable loss of weight."

"And were you present when she died?"

"No. And the night nurse was downstairs at the time. I was summoned immediately. Colonel Winthrop and Robert were in the room when I arrived. Everything possible was done to revive her."

"What time did you fix as the hour of death?"

"About 1:30 A. M. Taking into consideration the precipitable temperature of her emaciated body, I should say the time of death closely agreed with the nurse's report."

"And when was the body removed to the undertakers?"

"Colonel Winthrop can best answer that."

"Yes," the Colonel acknowledged. "They were notified immediately. The ambulance arrived shortly after daylight."

Huxford paused, his eyes almost closed.

"Dr. Judd," he questioned, "I presume you were absolutely positive in your diagnosis?"

The physician's eyes shifted.

"Why yes . . . yes," he faltered. "Yes and no. I found some parasites in her blood that bewildered me."

Huxford's eyes opened wide, then narrowed.

"What! You mean you suspect that she was infected with trypanosomes, the deadly parasites of the African sleeping sickness?"

Colonel Winthrop looked startled. "It seems impossible," he said. "That's a South African disease carried by the tsetse, a bloodsucking fly that bites in the day and in the full moonlight."

"Yes, *Glossina palpalis*," Huxford answered, "carrier of human trypanosomes."

The physician nodded. "That's right," he agreed and went on, "My microscopic examination of her blood definitely showed the parasites."

"And you falsely certified her death as encephalitis, the type of sleeping sickness known to this continent?"

"Yes," he admitted reluctantly. "Realizing that the disease was strictly foreign and that the tsetse fly could not survive our climate, I determined to decide in favor of my original diagnosis. I feared if the tropical disease were reported, the newspapers would make a sensation of it and bring undesirable publicity to the Winthrops."

The telephone jangled in the hall. Almost immediately the apathetic face of the butler loomed in the archway.

"A call for Mr. Robert!" he announced, making a half-bow.

Robert sprang to his feet. "I'll bet that's Kent now!" he declared, hurrying away.

A sharp silence fell over the room. Dr. Judd stirred restlessly in his chair, his steady eyes shuttling quizzically between Huxford and Colonel Winthrop. Walking heavily,

Robert returned. The color that had flushed his face a moment before had left it.

Dr. Judd looked up sharply. "What makes you so pale, my boy?"

Robert stared straight ahead. His face was grim, his lips quivered.

"What is it?" Colonel Winthrop demanded.

"Kent Jaimson is dead," he whispered.

"What!" stammered Colonel Winthrop. "Dead—?"

"Yes, his body was found early this morning."

"They don't think murder?"

"I don't know. That was his father. He said the police had found Kent dead in an alley on MacDougal Street. The body is at the Morgue."

Huxford rose, glanced at his watch, and turned to Robert. "Mr. Jaimson knew his son was with you last night?"

"Yes." He nodded nervously, lighting a cigarette. "That's the hell of it. I feel as if I were responsible."

"Of course, you explained that he left you and Miss Van Allen early in the evening?"

"Yes. But what if he . . .?"

"That's not to be considered at the moment," cautioned Huxford. "All you know is that Kent Jaimson left you and Miss Van Allen in front of the *Café des Artistes*. 'Football Hero Found Dead' will no doubt make the headlines for all the afternoon papers."

"Yes," Dr. Judd remarked, staring icily at Colonel Winthrop, "and if it's found he met with foul play, it'll make more than mere headlines."

Huxford again glanced at his watch. "If I hurry I can catch the express to New York. An unofficial visit to the Morgue may shed some light on the death of your friend."

"Wait!" Robert exclaimed, handing Huxford a card. "I almost forgot. It's the number of the taxicab Kent followed. I jotted it down."

9

EMERGING from the dimly lighted lower level of the Grand Central Station, Huxford strode into the bustling main concourse. From its high towering windows sunlight streamed down upon the hurrying throngs like a giant spotlight playing upon armies of pygmies. Swinging his Malacca cane, Huxford bored his way through the crowds of fur-coated women in pert bats, redcaps piled with luggage, pink-faced men like bears in bulging raccoon coats. He passed people staring hopefully as they waited around the fringe of the busy Information Booth and went under the broad arcade to the telephones.

Without losing any time, he called the Hack Bureau. In five minutes he had located the driver of the Jaimson cab and arranged for him to come to his office. Leaving the station on the Forty-Second Street side, he climbed into a taxi and ordered the driver to the Morgue. Weaving its way through the jumble of traffic, continuing under the rumbling Third Avenue El, the cab turned at Twenty-Eighth Street and sped toward the East River. High-stopped brownstone houses replaced red-brick tenements, ramshackle buildings loomed. Gaping signs across their dingy fronts proclaimed in lurid black letters: UNDERTAKER & SEXTON.

"Quite a flourishing business," commented Huxford to the taxi driver.

"Yeah," drawled the man, his cab careening out of the side street and sliding up to the curb in front of a high wrought-iron gate, "they're like a flock o' hungry buzzards waitin' for a carcass."

Slipping a bill into the driver's band, Huxford hooked his cane over his arm and climbed out of the cab. A building of worn brown masonry with tall windows and a façade of gray stone confronted him. In the background, in bold relief against the bleak sky, rose Bellevue Hospital, a rambling group of dull brick structures with tiers of built-in porches. Beyond, with its never-ceasing river traffic, its broken line of dwarfed buildings, its squatty docks, spanning bridges, and chugging tugboats, raced the sullen waters of the East River.

Stepping up to a cone-topped sentry box, Rex Huxford flashed his red police card. Behind a switchboard in a wide corridor of the mortuary building a girl in a starched blue smock chewed gum. At the side, a counter window labeled INFORMATION opened into an office. The metallic clatter of ticking typewriters, the jingling of phone bells, and the buzz of clerks moving about long rows of filing cabinets resounded in the vaulted hallway. A cluster of Horrid-faced men in trim black tailored overcoats, peaked at the shoulders and with satin-rolled collars, crowded about the counter window. One by one they edged up, scribbled on a form labeled "Undertaker's Permit," and scurried off down the corridor.

Huxford stepped up to the girl and showed his credentials. She glanced up curiously.

"Good afternoon," she mechanically greeted him, expertly plugging and pulling the long flexible cords of the switchboard. "Shall I announce you to the Chief Examiner?"

"Tell him I'll be downstairs," he replied. "It's not important."

She pressed a button. A thin man of medium height, his head shaved, looking in a white apron and a blue polo shirt like a man in an old-fashioned flannel undershirt with its sleeves clipped off at the armpits, popped through the door. A grimace twisted his taut, pasty dead-white face.

"Pedro, this is Dr. Huxford," the girl said between her operations at the switchboard. "Take care of him."

Gaping at Huxford, his mouth hanging open dumbly as though in a trance, the attendant led the way into the elevator; it descended slowly to the basement. The door slid open onto a dreary, silent white-tiled corridor, lined with rows and tiers of built-in compartments with protruding black panels like oven doors. It was cool, and damp with clinging drops of condensation. A slight sickly odor like the odor of narcissus pervaded the place. The wide passageway lined with vaults wound and then turned into a large, brilliantly lighted chamber. In the center of the marble floor was a tiled cubicle, its oblong glass windows suffusing a greenish light from a mercury lamp suspended over an operating table, about which hovered a group of men in white.

Huxford turned to the attendant, who had been silently staring at him. "I want to see the body of Mr. Kent Jaimson. It was brought in this morning."

"Yeah," the attendant grunted. "We've got 'im."

Shuffling across to a section of the mortuary vaults, he stooped down and squinted at a card framed in a slot on the frosted door of one of the compartments.

"Here's it," he mumbled. Straightening, he swung open the metal door and jerked out a sheeted body on a slab.

Huxford pulled back the canvas covering. Leaning over, he unhooked a white tag.

Replacing the tag, Huxford bent closer. He sniffed and detected a faint musty, arid odor. His eyes narrowed. As he had so often done in moments of close concentration, he hooked his left forefinger in the buttonhole of his coat lapel, then hastily withdrew it. He was trying to break himself of this habit. Bending closer he noted scarcely visible marks and bloodstains about the neck of the corpse. The minute lacerations were like the pitted marks resulting from abrasions made by falling upon sharp stones.

He nodded to his bilious-looking guide. The lackadaysical attendant wagged his shaven head; then, with a short thrust of his clubby foot, he sent the cadaver on its slab sliding back into its cold-storage cell, the door banging shut with a metallic thud. Huxford lit a cigarette.

"Pedro," he said casually, "I suppose the Morgue gets many bodies like this?"

"Yeah, plenty," the attendant answered callously. "In the spring when them Boaters blow in we gets more. Lately, we've been gettin' lots o' niggers."

Huxford blew a puff of smoke and flicked off the ashes of his cigarette.

"How do you account for that?"

"Yuh can't figure it. When yuh dealin' with tha public yuh never knows. Like Tony says fu his restaurant. Yuh can't figger what tha hell they goin' to do. When yuh ready for 'em they don't come an' when yuh ain't ready for 'em they crowd in on yuh. Yuh see we got er pool on tha stiffs. somethin' like playin' tha numbers. Each guy chucks er dime in tha pot an' puts down er number. Yuh can take tha ladies or gents. Niggers count nothin'—they're bad luck."

"Which do you play?"

"I takes tha ladies on holidays—we's gets more them times."

Huxford pointed his cane at a stack of small wooden cases piled in the corner of the chamber. "I see you have quite a number of boxes. Are those going out?"

"Yeah, them's goin' up tha river—Potter's Field. Got babies in 'em."

"Do you get that many every day?"

"Yeah, we gets more. People ain't got time these days fer raisin' kids. They drops 'em in ashcans, in the subways, an' in 'em sewers. Tha poor can't feed 'em an' the rich dames is' too busy runnin' around them swell joints. So we gets 'em."

"I don't suppose you run a pool on them, too?"

"Nah." He shrugged. "We don't count 'em. They ain't regular."

The muffled thud of a slammed door resounded. Huxford looked over his shoulder. A square-jawed, solidly built man, a gray Fedora pulled down over his steel-blue eyes, strode over.

"How are you, Professor?" he greeted Huxford gruffly. "I see Pedro's been entertaining you."

"Yes, Inspector." Huxford smiled grimly.

"Pedro's O. K.—he's just a little screwy," bantered Hogan. "Been with the Morgue twenty years. Used to be on the night watch, but he got drunk one time and mixed up all the stiffs."

Huxford's eyes twinkled. "He was telling me about the nice games they play here."

Inspector Hogan shoved his Fedora back. "The Medical Examiner tipped me off you were here," he said. "I was in the autopsy chamber. They just got through lakin' the guts out o' that Snyder fellow. Nothin' to it. His wife bumped him off with poison. All we need to cinch the case is the toxicology report, but I'll lay you two to one that dame won't burn. She'll probably beat the rap, and get one of them personal appearance contracts."

Shifting his cigar to the corner of his mouth, he asked, "You got anything hot?"

Huxford smiled deprecatingly. "No, I'm afraid not. I dropped in to look at the body of Kent Jaimson. I did so at the request of his friends."

Inspector Hogan straightened his Fedora. "Yeah, I know him. The big gridiron star. The body was finger-printed an' photographed in the Morgue line-up this mornin'. Looks like the guy was on a bender. Got hold of some bum booze. What do you make of it?"

"Nothing much." Huxford shrugged. "There are some suspicious marks about the body. Of course, they could have been the result of a heavy fall. Before I could be sure I would want to make a more thorough examination."

"Huh!" grunted the Inspector. "That's funny—it's the second stiff we've picked up this week in the Village. The other one's a dame, and not a bad looker either, for an unidentified. We're holdin' her cold storage pending action of the Missing Persons Bureau."

"You mean you found no clues that might lead to her identity?"

"Nothin' direct. All she had in her bag was a stick of chewin' gum, a lipstick, and sixteen cents. She must ha' been stinko. She was a swell dressed dame, but her clothes were dirty and torn from lying in the gutter. Only clue we found was in a pair of high-heeled shoes which had the trademark of a store out in Joplin, Missouri."

The Inspector took his thick cigar from the corner of his mouth and made a waving gesture. "Just another dizzy dame swallowed up by the Big City."

A tall gray-haired man with horn-rimmed glasses and wearing an immaculate white laboratory coat approached. He shook hands with Huxford.

"I would have come out earlier," he explained, toying with a pair of surgeon's gloves, "but I was tied up on a post-mortem. Is there anything we can do for you?"

"Yes, there is. I was telling Inspector Hogan about some very small marks and bloodstains I found on the body of Kent Jaimson. I'm a bit curious. However, they may be of no consequence."

"Good idea to find out. We'll take a look at him now," the Medical Examiner suggested. "The autopsy chamber is clear." He gave a curt order.

The three men entered the white-tiled room with its low hanging dome light and row of trough-like scrubbing basins. A strong odor of formaldehyde filled the chamber. A white-uniformed attendant wheeled in a covered body and slid it under the dome of the glaring operating lamp. In the greenish glow of the light the faces of the men looked a ghastly purple. Their figures as they bobbed about the compartment cast dancing shadows over its tiled walls and ceiling.

Huxford stood his cane in the corner with great care and hung up his tweed topcoat. He worked on a pair of surgeon's gloves, then with a magnifying glass proceeded to a minute examination of the body.

"There are many small wounds," he commented, without looking up. "Though contracted considerably, they seem to be oval in shape and look like those made by sharp teeth. Most of them are about the shoulder and neck."

Taking a scalpel, he probed dexterously into one of the minuscule wounds. His eyes narrowed.

"As I suspected," he said dryly, nodding to the Medical Examiner, who stood over him watching the proceedure. "These apparently innocent skin ruptures, you will note, are clotted punctures. Also, observe how they tap the arteries, and particularly those about the jugular. I don't recall seeing anything quite like it before."

"Yes," the Medical Examiner said, calmly nodding his gray head. "Looks like there's been a feast on blood."

"Precisely," agreed Huxford. "I hear you have another cadaver that was found in the same neighborhood under similar circumstances."

"Yeah—the dame," Inspector Hogan put in, "that 83-X holdover."

The Medical Examiner scowled, lifted the phone, ordered the female cadaver brought in. Huxford stepped up to a porcelain basin, rolled off his rubber gloves, and scrubbed his hands in mustard water. An attendant wheeled Jaimson's body out and returned with a sheeted corpse.

Inspector Hogan pulled back the covering, revealing the alabaster-white body of a young girl. Her well-rounded torso, with firm pointed breasts, was stretched out stiffly on the slab. It stood out like a classic figure sculptured in marble. Adjusting a magnifying glass to his eye, the Medical-Examiner leaned close over the corpse and squinted. Humming to himself, Huxford followed the examination. The Doctor straightened.

"The identical punctures!" he said, somewhat perplexed. "What does this mean?"

"It's evident that both parties were attacked in the same manner," Huxford stated. "Death ensued from exposure following excessive loss of blood."

A puzzled frown appeared on the Medical Examiner's face. "It's your belief, then, Dr. Huxford," he questioned, "that the deceased met death at the hands of some animal?"

"Yes," Huxford affirmed. "There is no other explanation. The minute nips, like sharp lancet teeth, I'm convinced are the marks of a bat—the vampire bat."

"Chrissssss . . . st!" ejaculated Inspector Hogan, shoving his Fedora back. "You mean we got one of them Draculas at large?"

Huxford smiled grimly. "Yes, I'm afraid so, and a very formidable one—*Desmodus rufus*, the vampire, a blood-sucking bat." he explained. "It attacks man and beast, and by its sharp lance-like teeth can easily open a vein and lap up blood."

"But New York isn't the habitat of the vampire bat!" declared the Medical Examiner, evidently incredulous.

"I'm quite aware of that," said Huxford. "Which leads me to believe we are dealing with more than a vampire—with a creature who employs the vampire in a ruthless quest for fresh young blood. A fiend whose habits are far more deadly than a Dracula."

"Looks like murder for blood," grunted Inspector Hogan. "I'd better put the heat on them Village joints."

"That appears to be the motive," Huxford agreed. "For the present, however, it would be better to keep this thing quiet. I believe it has been going on for some time. No doubt many bodies with the same marks have been brought in and unwittingly passed. I suggest the matter be kept to ourselves," he added, getting into his coat. "Any publicity at the moment would be a hindrance in solving the case and needlessly alarming to the public."

~§~

A zigzagging course in a rushing taxi past burdened trucks and tooting cabs brought Huxford to Rockefeller Center. A swift ascent to the sixtieth floor, and he was at his office. A swarthy, pitted-faced man, holding his cap in his hand, was smoking a cigarette in the reception room.

"Yeah, I remember the broad," the taxi driver said, dropping into a chair in front of Huxford' s desk. "A swell looker what gives me the creeps. Took her to West Sixty-seventh, and waited around that ritzy joint . . . Cafe somethin' or other. Art . . . Artist," he faltered.

"Said she was looking for a guy."

"And where did you pick her up?" Huxford asked.

"I was cruising around Thirty-fourth when she hopped my cab on the Avenue—near the Empire State Building."

"Did you notice anyone with her."

"Yeah she gave the cold shoulder to some palooka. A sawed-off gink in a black coat who scrammed when I pulled up. Them minked broads got no time for stiffs what try and make 'em on the street."

"How do you know that?" inquired Huxford.

"'Em china-faced dolls ain't runnin' around in a cab playin' the big time for nothin'. I've been rustlin' a hack too long, Mister. I know a chippy when I see one."

Huxford proffered the man a cigarette and took one himself.

"Tell me what happened to your fare," he said.

"Well, when the fall guy what she's got her lamps on comes out the swell joint, I starts up slowly. He tumbled for the dame's high sign-hopped a cab and followed. The guy musta been nuts for a sucker. He tailed us all the way to Washington Square."

"Greenwich Village?"

"Yeah," the taxi man drawled. Huxford narrowed his eyes. The driver continued:

"I rolled my hack up to a dark spot near the fountain. The other cah stopped in hack. She got out and I see the guy make her. The dame musta been in the dough. She slipped me a fin."

"You didn't see where they went?"

"No, sir. I pulled out with the other cah. I didn't see nothin'."

Huxford rose from his desk.

"I believe that'll be all," he said, pressing a bill in the man's hand. A black-haired girl, severely tailored, stepped into the private office.

"Mr. Robert Winthrop and Miss Van Allen are here," she announced. "And this cablegram just came."

"Thanks." He smiled as he took the blue envelope from his secretary. "You may show them in."

"Miss Van Allen, Professor Huxford," Robert introduced them.

"Won't you sit down, Miss Van Allen?" Huxford said, shoving up an upholstered chair.

"I'm most sorry to hear about Kent Jaimson," she said

in a slow, throaty voice, her lithe figure of exquisite grace as she turned with assured poise and sat down. "It was an awful shock."

Huxford dropped into his swivel chair and tilted back. After his gruesome visit at the Morgue the fresh radiant beauty of the girl was like a glow of sunlight. Her large turquoise-blue eyes, the lustrous honeyed hair nestling against the fine texture of her skin, the closeness of her vital loveliness set off by her clinging simple frock of emerald-green velvet, renewed within him a toxic sense of the beauty of life and at the same time confronted him with the disquieting realization of the fragile thread which held and separated life from death.

"Yes." He slowly nodded. "It's most disconcerting, I've just returned from making inquiries about the young man. Have you seen any of the newspapers?"

"We saw the headlines of the *Journal*. It's ghastly the way they're featuring it on the front page. They said he died of a heart attack-athletic heart."

"Well, that's something," Huxford said dryly. "It's a case of bad news turning out to be good news. I was beginning to fear they might play up the other angle. The police think he had been drinking heavily."

"What did you find out at the Morgue?" Robert asked.

Huxford glanced at him uncertainly, as if seeking some hint of procedure. "Why, er . . ." he faltered.

"That's quite all right," Robert said quickly. "You may talk freely. I've told Katherine everything. I felt it was best."

Her large blue eyes opened wide. "Yes, Robert has confessed. I think he should have told me before, don't you?"

"Of course," Huxford agreed. "I can see no reason why you shouldn't know. In fact, I was about to caution you both. I'm now convinced that Robert's every move is being watched. Apparently for some reason he holds the key to something vital. Kent Jaimson, I fear, was an unwitting victim."

"You mean he was murdered?" demanded Robert.

"Yes, brutally," Huxford replied. "After an examination of the body I'm forced to that conclusion. The police are working in the dark and as yet know nothing about this Schalkenbach. They've agreed to keep the whole matter quiet for the present. Undoubtedly, the Judas in the case is an enticing siren. A woman who lures young men to destruction . . ."

"Not Cynthia?" Robert blurted out.

Huxford slowly shook his head. "Yes, I'm afraid it's she. But a different Cynthia Winthrop than you knew. An eerie creature who is dead but at the same time not dead. A menacing creature, who is merely a pawn in an audacious biological experiment."

"Oh, how utterly horrible!" gasped Katherine. "I'm terribly frightened about Robert. I do hope he won't become involved. Isn't there something you can do, Dr. Huxford?"

Robert's face went pale. "Yes, for God's sake do something!" he cried. "We can't let this go on!"

Huxford looked up calmly. "This is not a time to get excited," he suggested quietly. "We've now established some definite factors and can proceed more confidently. The principal we're dealing with is too clever a strategist to become easily vulnerable. At present, I hardly believe he suspects we have knowledge of his grim undertaking. But I'm afraid it's only a question of time—we can't keep it from the police indefinitely."

He picked up the cablegram on his desk. "Perhaps this may shed some light," he said, slitting the envelope open. "It's a reply from a friend who is connected with the Gestapo, the German Secret Police."

He read aloud:

REXFORD   NEW YORK   EX-BERLIN ERIC
VON   SCHALKENBACH   BORN   DUSSELDORF
OCTOBER   25   1897   GRADUATED   HONORS
UNIVERSITY   HEIDELBERG   SPECIALIZED
SURGERY   KNOWN   AS   DUSSELDORF   GIANT   A
PRODIGY THE OFFSPRING OF FIRST COUSINS
LED RECLUSE LIFE SAILED TWO YEARS AGO ON
BREMEN   FOR   NEW   YORK   WHERE-ABOUTS
UNKNOWN SAID TO HAVE BEEN REMITTANCE
MAN EXILED FROM SOCIETY RECORD CLEAR
                                    MULLER

"Well," said Huxford, tossing the cablegram on his desk, "this at least confirms a statement I ventured at the Explorers Club. I said that he must be the result of a throwback brought about by close inbreeding. Nature's inexorable law of heredity. An extraordinary throwback, with the inherited characteristics of the powerful cave man of the Stone Age—not unlike the gorilla. A tragic form of retribution. Anachronistic, the case of a man born out of his time."

"Something like the monstrous creation of Frankenstein?" asked Robert.

The criminologist nodded. "But far more subtle. A giant man with prodigious intelligence and super-knowledge. A man with a hideous' physiognomy suffering from a severe persecution complex coupled with sexual repression, probably involving a neuropathic state analogous to dual personality. Perhaps mad."

10

THE slight warmth that precedes a snowfall descended upon the city. Large flakes began to fall in a silent profusion over Wall Street's darkened skyscrapers and deserted streets, which only a few hours before had been the animated scene of throngs of hurrying clerks and brokers. In the darkened canyon between towering concrete cliffs, a young man in gray topcoat and derby strode out of a building on upper Wall Street. He lighted a cigarette, looked about. Robert Winthrop was a solitary figure. Turning his face into the blinding snow, he groped his way past the marble façade of the Stock Exchange toward the Battery.

Alone in his office. he had constructed the chain of events leading up to the death of Kent Jaimson. Regretfully he had considered the fate that had befallen his friend. He still felt responsible for it. Perhaps he was being watched, if so, he would deliberately expose himself. He looked on this as no less than his duty. Determined to take the risk, he had slipped a pistol in his overcoat pocket.

At Bowling Green, he crossed the square. Battery Park, an expanse of barren trees and untrampled snow, stretched out desolately before him. Beyond, in the bleak swirl of falling snow blotting out the wide harbor, sounded the deep, intermittent bleat of foghorns.

From a dark side street emerged the hunched figure of a man. Robert's hand stole into his pocket. Red-eyed and coated with snow, the man squinted up from under his shaggy hat. Into his outstretched hand Robert dropped a silver piece.

"Luck, sir, an' God be with yuh," he mumbled between drooling lips, and shuffled away into the darkness.

Robert turned up Broadway, smiling a little as he reflected on the significance of the derelict's expression of gratitude. He regretted that he hadn't looked at the man's features more carefully. The dim yellow lights of an approaching taxi caught his attention. Out of the swirling snow it loomed, swung into a side street, and stopped for a moment. Then the clinking of its chains faded away in the distance.

"That's funny," Winthrop mused. "Someone got out of

that cab and disappeared in Trinity churchyard."

The neighborhood was deserted. Trinity Church, the proportions of its somber Gothic pile dwarfed by the surrounding buildings towering far above its spire, stood out like a lone sentry in a canyon of gray stone. Robert looked about, then walked along and ducked under the arched portal close to the dark wall of the church. Through the left-hand archway he peered out upon the yard of stubby-slabbed tombstones. In the snow, he noticed small footprints. They were evidently freshly made and led off into the graveyard. Hugging the walls, he traced them to the back of the church. Observing that the imprints circled the building, he quickly retraced his steps.

Out of the darkness something brushed against him. He stopped short in the shadowy vestibule. A huge shaggy cat with its back hunched, its fur bristling, and its tail straight up, hissed and spat at a dim figure in a darkened recess. Robert's eyes gradually became accustomed to the darkness. The figure, wrapped in a black cape, moved a little. Then it turned toward him. In the darkness, its eyes gleamed green like a panther's. The cat crouched, hissed, and let out an eerie cry. With a snarl, it sprang at the cloaked figure. The startled figure dodged back into the vestibule.

"Cynthia Winthrop!" gasped Robert.

"You weren't expecting me?" she said in a deep, hollow tone.

"It's the case of the stalker becoming the stalked," he answered, drawing his breath sharply. "I was afraid that beastly cat might claw your eyes."

"Cats—I loathe them," she said bitterly. "I could strangle them."

"But you were always so fond of animals. Have you forgotten how Chang would sit up for you—coyly cock her head and beg for sugar?"

"Don't speak of that," she retorted. "The past is dark. There are other things. . ." Her eyes were alight with a peculiar greenish hue. He had never seen anything like it before.

"But Cynthia . . . what is it? Aren't you—are you really my wife?" he finally ventured.

She stared at him in silence. Her eyes narrowed in cold, calculating appraisal. The church clock tolled the hour of midnight. Its melodious chimes reverberated solemnly through the darkened canyons.

"Yes," she answered at length after the last peal of the church bells faded. "Come with me."

Staring straight ahead, as though in a trance, she walked rigidly from the shadows of the portal. Her stiff black cape, broad at the shoulders and tapering toward her feet, suggested an old-fashioned coffin, standing upright with a head protruding from the top. They stood on the sidewalk, snow swirling about them. Pale flickering beams from the street lamp filtered through the white flakes upon them.

She turned her head toward him. The pallid light fell over her profile. Her immobile white face, with its deep-set black eyes with that greenish light, was like a death mask.

Robert experienced a thrill of adventure. He tingled with excitement as he thought of the extraordinary situation in which he found himself. The knowledge, however incredible, that the woman beside him was the same woman whom he had lost to death, and whom he had—or so he had believed—seen buried with his own eyes, was now beside him in the flesh in a strange reincarnation, was utterly incomprehensible. He was now more than ever determined to risk everything, if necessary, to fathom this enigma.

He hailed an approaching taxi, and helped her into it, following her.

"Washington Square!" she directed the cabman, before Robert could speak. The taxi lurched, its wheels crunching in the snow, it picked up speed.

"Cynthia, dear, tell me what has happened," he demanded, a tremor in his voice.

She drew up the high collar of her cape, shielding her ghastly face. Burying her head in its folds, she began to speak slowly in a deep throaty voice.

"You would not understand, I cannot explain . . ."

"But are you Cynthia Winthrop, my wife?"

"There's now a barrier between us. My marriage vows have been forfeited. Everything's so vague, so distant, so strange, as if I were living another life . . . like the baseless fabric of a vision—a breath of time . . .

A street lamp momentarily lighted the *tonneau* of the cab. Her pasty-white cheeks were sunken, her wheezy breathing was audible.

"Why, you are deathly ill!" he said in utter astonishment. "Shall we stop—call a doctor?"

Tenderly, he put his hand on her arm. Her flesh felt cold, like marble.

"Stop! Don't touch me!" she cried, recoiling from him and burying her head in the folds of her cape. "It's getting late . . ."

A sense of startled revulsion shook him. He felt weak, as though his vital energy were slowly being sapped by the closeness of her body. Beads of cold perspiration dampened his brow. A pungent, mousy odor, like the sickening odor of scorched human flesh, pervaded the stuffy cab. A white carnation in his lapel withered before his startled eyes.

"I'd better turn on the light," be faltered, groping for the switch.

"No! No! Not that!" she cried gasping for breath. Her voice sounded detached and far away, as if issuing from a sepulcher.

"Very well." The cab sped under the arch lit Washington Square. "Then I shall see you to your quarters."

The taxi slowed, the driver turned his head.

"Stop here!" Robert ordered, and they got out.

The snow-blanketed square with its stilled fountain and bare trees stood desolate before them. The prolonged whine of a hound baying rose and died. Swirling snow almost obliterated the rows of brick houses and massive apartment buildings overlooking the quadrangular park.

Cynthia's breathing became more labored. She hid her

face by holding the cape in front of herself. Panting, she suddenly turned upon him. Aghast, he swallowed twice and quickly drew away from her. Her panting faded into a rattle. It was a throaty, hollow sound, like a choking death rattle. Stealthily she approached him.

Stepping backward, he stared in terror. Her face had shrunk to the bony outline of her skull. Her long black eyebrows stood out sharply against her drawn, bloodless skin. Her black eyes, deep-set in her deathlike head, glowed green in the darkness as though phosphorescent. Again, that pungent odor assailed his nostrils. It was as stifling as sulphur fumes. Her black cape outspread, she edged toward him, her glazed eyes seeming to be floating in the darkness. Unable to move, he stared in fascinated horror. He sickened at the thought that his once lovely wife had become this creature. Far better that she were dead than this! The thought of what he ought to do began to run through his mind. He tried to consider the seemingly ludicrous consequence of a man's killing his already dead wife. Mindful that the exhumation had disclosed another woman's body, the possible outcome of such an act flashed through his mind. He attempted to imagine the legal complications that would follow and the serious predicament in which he might find himself.

His hand strayed to the gun in his pocket. He shuddered at the thought of what he might have to do. Seeking to frighten her, he drew his gun. Her thin lips twisted into a hissing rebuke. She came at him, her sharp teeth protruding like the fangs of a serpent, her cape glistening and outspread like the black-webbed wings of a scaly monster. Scarcely breathing, his finger stole to the trigger of the pistol as his trembling hand pointed the weapon at the strange, fearsome woman bearing down upon him.

At that instant, the lumbering bulk of a massive figure materialized out of the storm. The man was hatless, his bushy hair streamed down over his shaggy eyebrows and enormous wart-like face. His blubber lips set in a snarl, he reared like a monstrous bear above Robert. With a clawing sweep of his stocky arms he seized him, effortlessly he drew his body into the folds of his coat and carried him away as though he were a mere pygmy.

The sweetish odor of chloroform burned Robert's nostrils. He was vaguely conscious of a confused buzzing in his head, then everything was blank.

11

WITH a start Robert regained consciousness. His shirt open, his collar loose, and his hair disheveled, he sprang to his feet from the couch on which he had found himself. Dazed and sickened by the effects of the chloroform, he staggered to the center of the heavily carpeted room. In a peculiar purple light softly reflected from the high ceiling by hidden lamps, he gazed at the strange surroundings about him, bewildered. The walls were hung with curtains. Against one wall stood the couch. It was long and upholstered in leather with large cushions.

Vaguely the events of the night passed through his mind. The taxi ride . . . the horrible encounter with his tragically changed wife . . . his determination to shoot . . . the sudden attack . . . It was all like a dreadful nightmare. And now here he was in a soundproof chamber, presumeably a prisoner. By his watch it was exactly 1 A.M. If that was correct, he reasoned, he must have been unconscious at least thirty minutes. Then he could not be far from the scene of his abduction.

Going behind the heavy draperies where he saw streaks of light, he found what at first he thought was a window, but which proved to be only a recess suffusing a purplish glow. At the other end was a double sliding door, closed and locked. Behind the draperies he followed the wall and came to an arched opening which led to a hall with a wide stairway. At the end of the hallway I was a solid steel door, diagonally across which played a weird looking beam of greenish light.

He saw that it would be utterly impossible to reach the door without passing through the green beam . . . Suspecting that it was an electric eye that would set off an alarm if interrupted, he gave up the idea of going farther and retraced his steps. He noticed that his overcoat lay neatly folded on a chair near the couch. It puzzled him that someone had taken such pains. Suddenly behind him the draperies swished. Startled, he turned. An emaciated, yellow-hued man clad in a tight-fitting, high-collared mandarin robe with blue and white Chinese characters stood holding a tray.

"I am humble servant, Ying Tsung. I bring compliments of honorable master," he announced, pronouncing each word separately and distinctly. He set the tray of tea and crackers on a serving table, and bowed suavely.

"Distinguished guest enjoy hospitality of gracious master."

"I assume I am the guest of Dr. Schalkenbach?"

"He who knows few affairs of people has fewer troubles," the Chinese answered blandly.

Robert sat down near the tray while the expressionless Ying Tsung poured him a cup of tea. Raising the cup to his lips, he paused and scrutinized the enigmatic face of the Oriental.

The Chinese nodded.

"Everything fairly honorable, without trick or concealment," he said politely.

Sipping the tea, Robert inquired, "And what does your master, Dr. Schalkenbach, want with me?"

"Obedient servant most discreet like great master. Carry troubles in breast," he replied, clipping his words. "Man wishes that the boat he travels go faster—"

"Does your master intend to hold me?" demanded Robert.

"Man who catch fish must not mind getting wet," he replied in a provocatively reassuring tone, then slithered off, disappearing behind the draperies as quietly as he had come.

Undoubtedly Ying Tsung, Robert reflected, setting

down his teacup, was the same inscrutable Oriental who had accompanied Dr. Schalkenbach aboard the schooner in the Dutch Celebes. He vividly recalled his father's account of the missionary's voyage across the Java Sea and the strange happenings during the typhoon.

Feeling around in his pocket for cigarettes and not finding them, he went to his overcoat. He was startled to find his pistol. "Funny," he mused, quickly slipping it in his hip pocket. "How could it have been overlooked?"

Certain that Ying Tsung had gone, he crossed the room, determined to find what he could about the place in which he had been so comfortably made prisoner. Behind the curtains he discovered a small door like that of a closet. Cautiously turning the knob, he tried it. It creaked and stuck as if it had not been opened in some time. He stood still, listened. Slowly he drew the door open. Below the doorsill an iron spiral stairway dropped into a black void like a deep well. He edged himself through the narrow opening. At the bottom of the black shaft streaks of light came from what seemed to be crevices in a passageway.

Groping, he descended cautiously worming his way down the spiral stairway into a musty cubicle. Feeling his way along the cobwebbed walls toward the source of the pencil rays of light, he found a door, dropped on his knees, and squinted through the keyhole.

Part of a large laboratory, lighted by the mysterious purplish glow, shelves and stone-slabbed tables filled with assorted bottles, odd-shaped earthenware, batteries of distilling flasks, microscopes, and fuming chemicals—confronted his astonished gaze.

Held in fascination, he studied the room intently. Presently, the moving shadow of a bulky body and long arms spread grotesquely over the racks and the wall. Robed in a spotless white surgeon's gown, the massive figure of Dr. Schalkenbach loomed in front of a slabbed table. Overhead sputtered a globular pale-green light resembling a giant Rontgen tube. The doctor bent over a steaming retort. Straightening, he came up with a fuming test tube in his hand and held it up before his eyes. Then he turned his head and nodded.

Clad in a laboratory apron, Ying Tsung glided into view and shuffled off toward a row of heavy glass compartments the size of prison cells. Stepping up to each, he paused and intently inspected a dialed instrument.

Schalkenbach turned his bulbous face and muttered something to Ying Tsung. Of a sudden the Oriental snapped around and came straight for the door behind which Robert was concealed. Robert went quickly behind a concrete post and hid himself.

Ying Tsung flung the door open, the light flooded a dingy passageway piled with boxes. Scarcely breathing, Robert hugged the black shadow in which he was hidden. The Chinese stood silently framed in the threshold.

Conflicting thoughts troubled young Winthrop's mind. What did this mean? Had his presence at the door been detected? With a shudder, he recalled the missionary's story of what happened to the German skipper who had pried into Dr. Schalkenbach's affairs. For reasons which he sensed but could not express, he felt depressed, as though his life hung dangling in black space at the end of a single, taut thread which at any moment might snap.

The Chinese closed the door. There was a long, tense, silent moment. Robert remained motionless, listening. Finally, the metallic thud of a sliding bolt sounded. It clicked, locked.

Overwhelmed by the curiosity which prompted him to find out more about this laboratory, Robert again groped his way to the keyhole. Squinting through the narrow aperture, he saw Dr. Schalkenbach nod and mutter something to the Chinese, who slithered off, disappearing behind the high shelves of assorted chemicals.

Ying Tsung reappeared leading a blond young man who was naked to the waist. The Chinese led the pale trembling lad to one of the glass compartments at the farther end of the row. There was a wan, tense look on the boy's face. Dr. Schalkenbach reached up and pulled down a lever. The thick glass door slid open. A chorus of mingled squeaks and chirps rent the air. The blond youth shrank back. Dr. Schalkenbach leaned away from the lever. His huge hand went out, seizing the boy by the back of the neck, he thrust him into the compartment. A muffled scream of terror blended with the cacophony, then faded as the door slid shut.

Thinking of Kent Jaimson's fate and unnerved by what he had seen, Robert weakly crawled up the spiral stairway and threw himself on the couch. Apprehensive, he lay still. For some time, he gazed speculatively about the black curtained chamber with its strange purplish glow, which seemed to cast a baleful spell over the place.

Suddenly he heard the muffled music of a pipe organ playing *Die Meistersinger*. The heavy Wagnerian strains reverberated the room. The music rose, fell, and then culminated in its magnificent climax. Listening to the melody, played with a masterful touch, Robert wondered whether it was the habit of Dr. Schalkenbach to find solace in music after apparently using a human being for a guinea pig, much as Oliver Cromwell had found spiritual comfort in playing the organ after a sanguinary battle.

The music ceased. He heard the rumbling of a sliding door opening. The draperies swept out slightly and rippled as though fanned by a draft. A weak odor of antiseptic like the odor of carbolic acid scented the chamber.

The curtains parted. Bulging ungainly in a doubl-breasted coat and wearing a black ascot tie, his long bushy hair plastered behind his lobular ears, Dr. Schalkenbach hovered over him. He grinned down into Robert's face.

"So the lamb dropped into the tiger's mouth," he said in a patronizing tone. "It might have been quite embarrass-sing for you had it not been for my timely interference."

"Then it was you who brought me here?" Robert asked.

Dr. Schalkenbach fixed Robert with his black, hyp-notic eyes.

"I've been wanting to see you," he said in a more ami-cable tone.

"Then what do you want with me?" demanded Robert.

"I'm engaged in a biological experiment," he replied. "It's quite possible you can be a help to me. Your presence is very opportune—"

"I don't know what you are talking about," interrupted Robert. "Just what is the nature of this work you speak of?"

Dr. Schalkenbach's eyes flashed.

"Your experience tonight should have enlightened you."

"You mean that it concerns Cynthia?"

Dr. Schalkenbach grinned again, his irregular teeth showing.

"Cynthia Winthrop is dead," he stated emphatically.

"I thought so myself, until tonight," Robert's voice rose.

"Is that what you wanted me for—to tell me that?"

"I'm afraid you don't understand me," Dr. Schalkenbach answered condescendingly. "I've devoted many years to this experiment. My work, my music, have not been enough. They have only heightened my desire for the sympathetic love for life—for the association of lovely, cultivated women. I've been starved . . ."

"What has this to do with me?" Robert interrupted.

Dr. Schalkenbach's bulging black eyes flashed. "It has nothing to do with you," he replied quickly. "I might as well be frank. It's a psychological problem. I'm interested in the outcome of certain reactions of Cynthia Winthrop to you. Tonight, you became aware that she is no longer the woman you knew. She is now Desmodus—Desmodus the Princess."

Robert's voice faltered. "But what have you done to her?"

"She once loved you," Dr. Schalkenbach went on with a trace of bitterness in his voice. "I wanted to test her mental reaction."

"You mean you've made her an automaton," broke in Robert. "How can you be so inhuman—use her as a guinea pig?"

Dr. Schalkenbach looked at him sharply.

"Not in reality," he replied curtly. "But you've no grounds of complaint—you have . . . Miss Van Allen. I'm sure you wouldn't want anything to happen to your—" he sarcastically emphasized the word— "charming Katherine Van Allen?"

His eyes glared down at Robert. "I'm not going to stand for any interference. My work must go on." His voice rose. "Nature has molded me in this misshapen shell. I shall fight nature—make a woman finer than man has ever known, a woman who will inspire me to even greater heights." He doubled his massive fists, his chest swelled. Through my achievements a better race will come about," he roared. "I shall startle the scientific world . . . I shall have accomplished something no scientist dared attempt. Great universities shall confer degrees upon me, the Royal Academy will know me. I shall control the fate of mankind. I shall be the great Schalkenbach . . . the finite creature who defied the Infinite."

Bowing awkwardly, he turned and abruptly lumbered out of the room. Exhausted and weary, Robert dropped back onto the couch. Once more the deep tremolo of the organ surged through the room. The riotous strains of Mephistopheles' song of triumph rose and fell. Then, at length, the melody trailed off as the purplish glow that suffused the chamber faded into darkness.

Robert lapsed into a semi-torpid state, vaguely disturbed about his fate. Snatches of Dr. Schalkenbach's bombastic ravings, his mad ambition, flitted across his tormented mind. In his half-conscious sleep he heard a voice. "Take him . . . he is yours," the voice urged in a whisper. He felt the presence of someone in the room. The voice whispered again, more insistently. He awoke with a start, listened. The chamber was still darkened except for a dim glow in the far corner of the high ceiling. Lying on his back, his eyes wide open, and convinced that his mind had played him a prank, he drifted off again into vague, confused consciousness. As if in a dream he saw slowly approaching him two green spots glowing like coals of fire. His arms felt numb and heavy. He tried to lift them and could not. The phosphorescence hovered over him. Once more he heard the voice whisper. This time it was clear and distinct. The glowing spots became two glaring, luminous eyes.

Reaching for his pistol, he sprang to his feet. And without thinking he put the gun before him and blindly pulled the trigger. Five staccato explosives broke the silence. The figure stood motionless. From above a purple beam of light flashed on and played down. Cynthia, enveloped in the spotlight, her face full but pale, her loveliness restored, stood facing him, clothed in a black velvet gown. She was staring straight ahead, like a sleepwalker. In the fringe of the purple beam, a sardonic grin on his nodular face, Dr. Schalkenbach looked on.

"A bit reckless, aren't you?" he said caustically. "You don't think I'd leave a loaded gun . . .? Those shells were blanks." He broke into a deep guttural laugh.

12

JAGGED blocks of ice glistening like jewels in the placid sound drifted in the distance past the bay window. The ice-crusted snow brilliantly reflected in the morning sun brightened the somber Gothic drawing room. In a rich dressing gown, his face drawn, his eyes swollen, and drawing nervously on a cigarette, Robert paced the Boor.

"And you say you found yourself on Tenth Street near the Sixth Avenue El?" Huxford questioned.

"I was left near the basement door of a boarded-up brownstone house," he explained. "As soon as I dared, I took off the blindfold and looked to see in what direction Ying Tsung had gone. But it was snowing hard and I couldn't distinguish anything."

"Could you estimate the number of steps you were led down?" Huxford continued his questioning.

"I was carried down. I'm quite certain it was Dr. Schalkenbach who did it. When we got down on the side.

walk, I think he left. Then, Ying Tsung locked his arm in mine and led me through the streets. I was so well blindfolded I couldn't see a thing. We circled and turned so much that I have no idea where we went."

"How long do you think you were walking?"

"It seemed about twenty minutes. Of course, it could have been much less. As soon as my eyes became accustomed to the light, I looked at my wrist watch under a street lamp. It was running, but I knew it had been tampered with. The hands showed after nine. When I found a taxi, the driver told me it was ten minutes after five."

"Did Dr. Schalkenbach make any threats."

"Yes, before I was blindfolded he said that if I spoke of my experience, I would pay. He implied that something would happen to Katherine."

"You're to be congratulated that you weren't detained indefinitely," Huxford said, dryly. "You might have met the fate of Kent Jaimson and the young Nordic."

"You didn't say anything to Dr. Judd this morning?" Colonel Winthrop asked his son.

"No, I thought it best not to. He gave me a sedative to quiet my nerves and made a crack about young men who stay out all night."

Robert continued to pace the room. "But we must do something about Cynthia," he insisted. "We can't let this madman go on."

"You must have patience," Huxford said quietly. "We're acting alone in this matter, and our problem isn't exactly a simple one. Did you notice anything about

Schalkenbach's quarters—anything that might help us?"

Robert paused in his pacing. "In the hall was a wide, old-fashioned stairway—the ceilings were unusually high. When I looked out into the hall I saw a steel door at the end of it. Everything was so eerie I could make out very little."

Huxford slowly shook his head. "It's quite clear Dr. Schalkenbach's locale is in the neighborhood of Washington Square," he said. "I'm convinced the end of our quest is within the radius of two blocks of the place where you were abducted.

"Your remark about the high ceiling indicates that the house in which you were a prisoner is a remodeled brownstone of the early eighties. By elimination, therefore, and from my general knowledge of the neighborhood, I should say offhand that it sifts to one out of a possible two hundred of this type of dwelling. The fact that you were carried down the steps would suggest some unusual characteristic, such as a high or steep stoop, which Dr. Schalkenbach wanted to conceal."

"Then why should he be so careless as to leave his victims so close to the scene of the crime?" Colonel Winthrop asked.

Huxford smiled faintly. "I don't think he did. I'm of the opinion he doesn't leave his victims where they are found. From the examinations I made at the Morgue, I'm quite certain Jaimson and the woman there were let out in a dazed condition and wandered away of their own accord. It was a clever stratagem to let his victims, weakened by loss of blood and partially deranged, stagger about like drunkards only to collapse and die of exposure.

"His scheme has evidently been working very well for some time. As I pointed out to the Medical Examiner, possibly hundreds of bodies with the vampire marks have unsuspectingly been passed, death being ascribed to natural causes."

Robert abruptly stopped his pacing and faced Huxford.

"You surely don't think that?" he exclaimed incredulously.

"I'm afraid so."

"Then why did he let me go?"

"Undoubtedly he wanted to see what effect your presence would have on your wife. He hoped the shock would bring about an emotional crisis that would help her. He was afraid to harm you, as her reaction might be disastrous." Huxford looked up at Robert appraisingly.

"If you had been just a wee more robust and fleshy young man," he said with a faint smile, "we might be looking for you this morning. But I don't think so."

The Colonel spoke up. "How do you think Dr. Schalkenbach acquired all his wealth? I understand your cabled information stated that he was a remittance man."

"You'll recall, Colonel, how the Indians of the Amazon country worshiped him as a white god?" Huxford replied. "This unquestionably made it possible for him to move about the jungles freely. The soldier of fortune, Pat Morgan, who boasted of an El Dorado abounding in platinum was lost. But Dr. Schalkenbach was more successful in getting what he went after than your Captain Sheldon's red-bearded friend. If Dr. Schalkenbach did get his hands on this particular source of platinum, he's more than well off, he is rich.

"I once heard an English mining engineer say that the metal was so common there that the Indians, unaware of its value, had fashioned crude utensils out of it." He smiled slightly. "I wouldn't be surprised if we found that some of Dr. Schalkenbach's wealth was in the form of pots and pans."

"What are you going to do about Schalkenbach?" asked Robert.

"I've a number of leads which may be of benefit in locating his hiding place. It will take at least twenty-four hours to check the necessary information. In the meantime, let's hope he doesn't get wind of our activities. If he does, it will prove a serious setback."

"How on earth do you account for Cynthia's strange condition?" asked Robert. "And the ghastly purplish light?"

"Your once lovely wife has become the pawn in a biological experiment," Huxford replied. "I'm convinced that we have to cope not only with the cunning strategy of a mad scientist, but with an extraordinarily delicate problem. I believe the transformation you saw," he went on, "is affected by the devitalization of the blood corpuscles, a complete breakdown of the cells, with a total loss of vital energy, analogous to a form of starvation.

"In Cynthia's case, it would seem that the recharging

agent is fresh young blood. In her present stage of vampirism, blood is perhaps the only form of nourishment she is capable of assimilating. Her strange revulsion to light, I venture to say, is caused by a peculiar biological condition. The normal vibrations of white light have an irritating, perhaps a destructive, effect on her bodily tissues. The purplish glow that so fascinated you is used, I believe, to neutralize this abnormal condition.

"Perhaps we shall find, if we're fortunate enough to locate this laboratory, that this peculiar light which suffuses his quarters is normal light with certain injurious bands filtered out. It's my theory that the light may be similar to a combination of the infrared and Rontgen rays. Sunlight, or ordinary incandescent light, apparently has a tendency to dissociate or break down the blood cells, and is a contributing factor in the revolting transformation which you witnessed. It's obvious that the purplish glow prevents the dissociation of the cells and brings about what is known in biochemistry as ionization. We might compare the biological action in a general way to the charging and discharging of a storage battery."

"You mean that in order to live, she's dependent upon this purplish light?" demanded Robert, settling down on the arm of a chair.

"The direct rays of the sun would probably terminate her present existence. If we're not too late, a light ray may prove our most effective weapon."

"The lethal ray?"

"No, hardly. A lethal ray, at least those I've seen

demonstrated for war purposes, is invisible. The ray I contemplate would be a bright white light with all the colors of the spectrum."

"Then how about the light of the full moon?"

"She has become a strictly nocturnal creature. In all probability she sleeps in the day and can only come out at night. The soft beams of the moon may be a tonic to her and even act as a magnet to attract her."

"Like the bat!"

Huxford nodded. "Yes, I don't like to make the comparison, but I'm afraid that's pretty much the case. With this difference, that bats are attracted by light, and of course it's not harmful except as it lures them to their doom."

The Colonel interposed. "Schalkenbach then has ironically enough, given her an appropriate new name?"

"Yes, *Desmodus rufus*, as you probably know, is a neotropical, bloodsucking bat, whose habitat is chiefly Central and South America."

"Can you tell me, then," Robert asked, "why Cynthia was so repulsed by the cat?"

"Perhaps she has something of the feline in her," replied Huxford. "Her changed personality, having taken on some of the characteristics of a wild animal, was sensed and resented by the cat. Animals, as you know, in comparison to mankind, have a keen sense of smell, to compensate for their inferior eyesight. This sense enables them to smell faint odors that man cannot detect.

"People who have an innate dislike or fear of animals

particularly dogs and cats, even though they betray no external sign, involuntarily give forth an excretion to which the animals react. This is exactly what happened in the churchyard. Since your wife has become the victim of vampirism, her presence could be sensed at a considerable distance. She has become the type of creature that would cause a hound to bay."

"I shall never forget bow gruesomely her eyes lit up," Robert said with a shudder. "Could there be a relation between this and her other abnormalities?"

"I believe so, but it's all rather involved. Very little is known about the cause of luminosity. It's mostly found in animals, and occasionally in certain plants. At one time, I did a little investigating of light-producing insects.

It may interest you to know that all such insects are nocturnal. Everyone is of course familiar with the firefly, commonly known as the lightning bug, which emits a greenish-white phosphorescent light. There's also a beetle found in South America which is quite extraordinary. This precautious, law-abiding, chubby little beetle flashes a red light at both ends of its body, and green lights along its sides—it almost meets a maritime regulation.

"I also acquired some specimens of the Cuban beetle known as the *cucuyo*. Unlike its meticulous cousin of the port and starboard variety, it carries only too yellowish eyelike 'lamps' on each side of its head. In the darkness at a distance they resemble the headlights of a motorcar. In Cuba, we called it the automobile bug.

"The luminosity so generated is a form of electrolysis

that causes putrefaction. It's really a photogenic substance thrown out from the body, which becomes luminous when in contact with the oxygen of the air. The only reason I could find why these insects require a light was that in producing it they throw off an odor which serves as a weapon of defense. Some species of the bat feed upon these insects, but frequently they are repelled by this odor.

"I have observed further that it's a peculiarity of many animals that their eyes glow in the dark. Since your wife has acquired some of these characteristics, it would not be unnatural for her eyes to take on this idiosyncrasy. I should also say that she has acquired the ability to dilate the pupils of her eyes to a high degree like a cat.

"A case recorded by Commander Kane, an Arctic explorer, on his last trip to the polar region, mentioned the singular phenomenon of a human body becoming luminous a short time before death. And in some instances the eyes have been known to become phosphorescent for a considerable time after death."

Huxford paused. "The irritating odor you described as of scorched flesh," he went on, "was brought about by the gradual dissociation of her blood cells which I spoke of. Her labored breathing produced something quite Similar to perspiration, which induced putrefaction. Cut flowers, as you already know, are extremely sensitive to putrefaction. It was this, of course, which, seemingly so mysterious to you, wilted your carnation. I know of an instance in which flowers withered almost at once in the presence of a corpse, even though there was no perceptible odor to the human sense of smell."

"It's not a pleasant comparison you draw . . . a living corpse!" Robert muttered, the blood leaving his face.

The Colonel abruptly looked up. "What do you think about Dr. Schalkenbach?" he asked. "It seems incredible that only two men can be involved in this."

"I doubt if he has any direct accomplices other than Ying Tsung," Huxford answered. "The Chinese appears to be very clever, as you might expect. It was he, I'm sure, who kept Dr. Schalkenbach informed regarding your son's movements. I don't doubt that the footprints Robert saw in Trinity churchyard, and thought were his wife's, were in reality Ying Tsung's. A conspicuous man like the doctor wouldn't be apt to appear in public. Undoubtedly, he goes out occasionally late at night. But I'm sure he's just a bit wary since his appearance at the opera."

"In what manner does Cynthia take the blood?" asked Robert bluntly.

Huxford frowned slightly. "I hope to have something important to tell as to that after I visit the Academy of Medicine. It may be tonight. I might explain," he added somewhat reluctantly, "that the young Nordic whom you saw forced into the glass compartment doubtless served the purpose of a most inhuman sanguinary feast and—"

"Pardon me, sir," the butler interrupted, standing in the doorway and addressing Colonel Winthrop, "Professor Huxford is wanted on the telephone."

"I left word at my office I'd be here," Huxford explained, striding out of the room.

Robert rose from the arm of his chair and turned to face his father.

"Can it be possible that Cynthia is taking blood from these men?"

"That's a matter for Dr. Huxford. I think we'd better drop the subject," the Colonel replied with finality.

Huxford returned to the room frowning.

"Well, the cat's out of the bag," he announced. "That was the New York police—Inspector Hogan of the Homicide Bureau."

"You mean the police know?" asked the Colonel

"They've found another body," he replied briefly. "The Inspector wants to see me." Huxford paused his eyes narrowed slightly as he faced the grave stare of Colonel Winthrop. "I don't want to be an alarmist, but it might be a good idea, as a precautionary measure, to invite Miss Van Allen to stay here for the next few days. I also suggest that you get a guard to patrol the grounds."

13

THE reception room of Huxford's small office hummed with the casual conversation of reporters and photographers restlessly awaiting his appearance, an occasional boisterous voice rising above the chatter. Cigarette smoke hung over the room. Perched on the edge of the reception desk, Inspector Hogan, a chubby cigar working in the corner of mouth, his gray Fedora pulled down over his forehead, scowled at the men elbowing about him.

"Pipe down!" he snorted, waving them away. "You'll get your break. I'm not letting nothin' out till I talk it over with the Professor. Last time you guys busted in, I shot my trap. And the Chief's still squawking."

"Yeaaa-ah!" a reporter drawled. "But look what a swell build-up we gave you?"

A short man called over the shoulders of the others, "How long's the Commissioner been holding back on this story?"

"The Chief got it from the Med at the Morgue. But don't quote me. Between us, I'm a little sore."

"Who broke the story, then?" bantered another reporter.

The inspector grinned sheepishly. "This feller Huxford pulled a fast one—got wind of it and hushed it up."

"What's the big idea, Hogan?"

"You got me, boys," he answered, shoving his Fedora back and mopping his brow.

"If there's anything to this, it'll bust the papers wide open," remarked a reporter from the *Mirror*.

The door from the corridor opened. The talking ceased abruptly. A very little man, a package snugged under his arm and holding on to an umbrella, edged through the door. The newspapermen eyed the man quizzically.

"What—a delivery?" a ruddy-faced reporter inquired.

"I am Mr. Skeets. I'm from the *Bronx Home News*,"

the man announced. "I've come to interview Professor Huxford." A rousing cheer went up, punctuated by a razz.

"The *Bronx Home News* covering this? It must be hot," a reporter shot.

"Who told you there was a Bronx angle?" loudly joshed another.

"They must be in the know," said someone laughing.

"Gentlemen," Mr. Skeets from the *Bronx* retorted with injured dignity, "I would have you know one of the reputed victims of the bat resided in the Bronx."

A laugh swept the room.

"A reporter from the *Journal* turned to the Inspector. Yeah—and they tell me at the Morgue the All-American star, Kent Jaimson, pal of young Winthrop was another victim. How about that, Hogan?"

"What!" the Inspector croaked. He bit savagely into a fresh cigar and mumbled something incoherently.

"What's the matter, Inspector? Got a fresh idea?" Asked a Hearst man.

"I was thinking."

"What, again?"

"Cut them wisecracks," he snorted. A friendly snicker ran around the room. "Gentlemen of the press, gentlemen," sarcastically demanded the Inspector, "quiet, *pleassssse!* We must have dignity here."

"Come on Hogan, be a good fellow. Open up—give us a lead on the bat murders. It'll put you in the limelight," cajoled the Post reporter. "We've got a deadline to meet."

"I told you nothin' doing till I see the Professor."

"So the Police Department are passing the buck too!" jibed a newshawk.

"Hell! You fellows are never satisfied. I tell you—"

The door opened. In a camelhair coat, his Malacca cane hanging on his arm, Huxford strode into his office. The newspapermen clamored around him.

"Just give me a little time, boys, and I'll try to answer your questions," he greeted them, pushing his way through. Pausing at the door of his private office, he beckoned to Inspector Hogan.

"The Chief's got me on the spot," the Inspector began as soon as he closed the door. "Cripes! They're raisin' holy hell. The Medical Examiner refuses to keep the lid down any longer. He's spilled everything. It's makin' a goat out of me."

"Just what's happened?" Huxford asked, tilting back in his swivel chair.

The Inspector shifted his cigar to the other corner of his mouth and rested his weight on the edge of Huxford's desk. "They've found another stiff in the village," he said rapidly. "A young Danish guy's got the marks of the bat. Before I could get to my desk this morning, the Medical Examiner passed the buck to the Chief. A couple of them wise cracking newshawks bangin' around headquarters got wind of it and blew the case. And it looks like I'm the goat."

"I take it, then," Huxford remarked calmly, "that the Commissioner knows of my interest in the matter."

"Yeah, the Med tipped him off. Said you're holdin' out

on us."

"What are their intentions in the case of Kent Jaimson?"

"That's the stink in the bag," the Inspector answered. "He was too big a shot to pass up. Finding this Danish guy, with that good-lookin' dame from Joplin in cold storage, busted the case wide open."

"Did you look at the body of this Dane?"

"Yeah, he's at the Morgue. Full of them bat marks. And I'll bet there ain't a pint of blood left in him."

"In what part of the Village was the body found?"

"According to the morgue tag he was found at 6:10 A.M. near the southeast corner of Washington Square. The patrolman in the precinct said the body was sprawled out in the snow—"

"Was there anything to identify him?" Huxford broke in.

"A wallet with about ten bucks. They searched for identification papers but found nothin'. But he was identified this morning. Some cousin from the Bronx called the Missing Persons Bureau. Seems the guy had been away for two days.

"I had one of our men up in the Bronx hop over and see the woman. He phoned me, said the guy was A.B. on one of them Swedish-American boats. He'd been on a party two nights before with this cousin and her boyfriend. She claims they had just come out one of them Bavarian joints on Eighty-sixth street when a good-looking dame comes along in a taxi and picks him up. That was the last they saw of him. She said he'd been drinking. She was worried because he didn't show up. What rubs me some reporter scrams up there before our man could cover. He got some screwy story tyin' up the dame in the taxi with them bat murders.

"This's got me up a tree," he admitted, scowling. "They're puttin' the heat on me. I've got to make a showin' with the newspapers blowin' this for a big case. Fourteen years on the Department," he lamented, "and a crazy case like this handed me!" He pushed his Fedora back bit savagely on his cigar. "I tell you it's got me.!"

"I regret that it had to break wide open," Huxford said. "I was hoping we could keep it under cover."

"I'm sorry Professor, I did my best."

"Well, Hogan, what are you going to do about it?" Huxford challenged, his eyes twinkling. "Going to make a quick arrest?"

The Inspector grinned deprecatingly. "I know, Professor, you've got the drop on me. But how about young Winthrop?" he demanded. "You just came from there. What's he got to say?"

"Look here, Hogan," Huxford replied sharply, "if you're going to play ball, I want you to let me handle the Winthrops. I don't want any of your men going out and bothering them. Do you work with me?"

"Don't get me wrong, Professor," Hogan blustered. "Sure, I work with you."

Huxford leaned slightly forward, looked intently into the Inspector's cold, steely eyes. "I should like you to handle this, Hogan," he urged in a slow deliberate voice. "It can be a big feather in your cap. I prefer to remain in the background."

"It's a deal!" the Inspector quickly agreed. "When do we get goin'?"

"We'll discuss that later. It's not well to keep newspapermen waiting. When they've gone, we'll go over the case."

"O. K., Governor—you've got the layout," the Inspector said, tilting his cigar arrogantly in his mouth.

Huxford pressed a button on the side of his desk. "Tell the boys to come in," he said, addressing his secretary. The newspapermen milled into the office and crowded around Huxford.

"Take it easy, boys," barked the Inspector, still perched on the desk. "Wheredya think you are—the subway?"

"All right, gentlemen," Huxford said. "One question at a time."

"How long have you been holding back on this?" a reporter demanded.

"I've nothing to hold back. This is the first time been interviewed." Huxford laughed. "I believe Medical Examiner has given yon boys a fair account."

"Yeah—but what is your opinion of these murders?"

"They were the mark of a female vampire, the tool of a Dr. Schalkenbach."

"How do you know that?" demanded the *Tribune* reporter.

A faint smile played about the corner of mouth. "I've

been quietly working on this for days. My information comes from a confidential source."

"So this Schalkenbach," said the *Mirror* reporter, a Svengali with a Trilby?"

"You're getting pretty hot," replied the criminologist.

"What can you tell us about this vampire?" the man from the *News* shot. "How do you explain those markings?"

"Is this dame a bat woman?" said someone, with snicker. A laugh ran around the room.

"Unquestionably," Huxford stated with dignity, deaths were caused by the incisions of sharp lancet and are definitely the work of the vampire bat."

"What sort of a looking guy is this?" broke in the *Journal* reporter.

"I understand," Huxford replied, "that he's a massive, misshapen German. A scientist with a nodular face, endowed with superintelligence. A man whom once you saw you could never forget."

"Like a bloated water bag with warts?" cracked the newshawk from the *Mirror*, scribbling on the back of an envelope.

"What clues have you?" abruptly asked the Tribune reporter.

"We've gathered a few threads, so to speak, which may lead to an early arrest."

"What do you mean, early?" persisted the Tribune man. Huxford smiled deprecatingly. "It's entirely in the hands of the Police Department. Inspector Hogan, I'm sure, will let you boys in on it when the time comes."

"Is it true, Professor Huxford, that you are in the pay of a socially prominent family to squash a scandal?" asked the *Journal* reporter.

"There's absolutely no truth in that," denied Huxford coolly. "I'm merely acting in an advisory capacity. The honors," he added, nodding to the Inspector, whose weighty figure sat stolidly on the edge of the desk, "must go to Inspector Hogan of the Homicide Bureau. I'm sure his contributions to this case will be not only a great help toward its solution but also a credit to the Police Department."

The Inspector swelled visibly.

"A pretty little speech, Huxford," retorted a cynical newshawk. "Isn't it true," he added, abruptly turning to the Inspector, "that the Commissioner had you on the mat this morning and threatened a shake-up for your negligence in stalling the investigation?"

"Naw, there's nothin' to that!" Hogan growled out of the corner of his mouth. "You guys gotta pipe down. The Chief and me are on the best of terms.

"All right Hogan, we'll skip it."

"What kind of a looker is this bat woman?" queried the *News* reporter.

"Attractive enough to lure susceptible newspapermen," Huxford replied with a touch of jocularity.

"*Yeaaa-ah?*" derided a chorus.

"What sort of sex life does a vampire lead?" fired the man from the *Mirror*.

"Not unlike the desires of those practicing the frenzied rites of voodooism, her sexual desires are satisfied by an orgy of blood."

"A bloodthirsty sadist," muttered a voice in the back of the room. "Think of a man in love with a living corpse!"

A reporter impeccably attired in a dark-gray suit and bowler stepped up before the desk. "Would you be kind enough to give me a special interview?" asked the *Times* scribe with an air of aloofness. "Our readers like the scientific viewpoint."

"I'll be glad to accommodate you later." Huxford rose, thumped a cigarette, and lighted it. "If there's anything else we can do, boys . . ."

"Just a minute!" shouted a photographer, elbowing his way forward. There were two flashes. The newspapermen filed out.

Dropping back into his chair, Huxford leisurely drew on his cigarette. Inspector Hogan straightened his hat, leaned over the desk.

"Holy mackerel!" He scowled as the last sounds of departing reporters trailed off. "We got one of them unbalanced egotists . . ."

"He's a tough hombre, Hogan. It won't be easy. He's got a hideaway like a fort."

The Inspector bristled. "Leave that to me. We'll blast 'em out." Lowering his voice, he added in a more sober tone. "You're sure workin' inside this case, Governor. What's the hot leads?"

Huxford calmly blew a puff of smoke, his eyes twinkling. "Yes, Hogan," he replied, "as I stated at the Morgue, my knowledge of the case convinces me that our man is in the neighborhood of Washington Square. The places where all the bodies have been picked up, if plotted, would converge on a spot within an area of two square blocks of that vicinity."

The Inspector shoved his gray Fedora back. "Say, Governor," he interrupted, leaning forward inquisitively, "it ain't none of my business, but what's this Goddamn bat woman?"

Huxford smiled benignly. "That, Inspector, involves a rather elaborate experiment in biology," he explained. "The vampire was once a lovely woman who died in a manner from a malady not usual in this country. It was almost a year after burial that her astounded husband saw her from a distance at a performance in the Metropolitan. She was in the company of this Dr. Schalkenbach. And later I was told by the unnerved husband the horrifying story of his encounter with his changed wife."

"Humm," murmured the Inspector. "He must have been a Mary Warner dope."

"Hardly," Huxford replied. "His mental attitude was not that of the marihuana smoker. That drug produces more of the hallucinations of floating. Unlike the effects of other narcotics, the marihuana user finds ideas crowding one another with such rapidity that his speech is unable to keep pace with his lightning thoughts. At first, I suspected his story might be a fantasy induced by morphine. But later events have led me to believe otherwise."

"O. K., Professor," said the Inspector. "But how about this Dr. Schalkenbach's hide-out?"

"I have reasons to believe," Huxford replied, "that his house is a brownstone with a high stoop. The interior has been remodeled. Steel doors have been built in—no doubt concealed behind the frame doors."

"Cripes, Governor, there ain't more than sixty of them old houses left in the neighborhood. If you say so, I'll plant a squad down there."

"I doubt whether this Dr. Schalkenbach will show himself, especially after he sees the evening papers. But he has a shrewd lieutenant, a Chinese, who will probably go out at night. I think you had better have your men watch for this Oriental. After tonight he'll unquestionably resort to some disguise."

"Yeah," agreed the Inspector, "I'll get the boys to bring him in and I'll clout the livin' hell out of him. I can make them Chinks talk."

"That sort of thing won't go any more," Huxford remarked dryly. "The thing to do is make a survey of the neighborhood—check all leaves. That shouldn't take long, as most of the houses there are owned by the people who live in them. Of course, you won't find any lease registered under the name of Schalkenbach, but you may find something suspicious. In any event they'll be forced out sooner or later. To live, the vampire must have fresh blood."

14

SCHALKENBACH'S massive figure swayed, his head bobbed. His hands effortlessly moved from manual to manual, his fingers deftly played from key to key, while a large hand occasionally reached out to close or pull a stop. His legs, pumping like eccentric pistons above the pedals and keys, was completely absorbed in the swelling strains of *Die Meistersinger's Prize Song* as the measures burst into their fullest pomp and glory.

The organ, on a dais at the end of the vaulted chamber, was partly concealed by rich black velvet draperies. Between the parting of velour curtains was revealed an inner room, in which the two stately posts of a canopied bed were visible. Like moonbeams, purplish rays streamed between the divided curtains, lighting the music chamber in a subdued glow and casting grotesque shadows of Dr. Schalkenbach's swaying bulk upon the walls.

He looked up at himself in the oblong mirror above the keyboard. He gazed into it. His reflected countenance glared hideously back at him. His hands dropped to the choir manual. The tones lightened and then softened.

"Almighty, incomprehensible riddle unfathomable mystery," he droned, as if praying to himself. "Why have You so ironically given me this shape?" he challenged his Maker. "Does it not belie me?" His huge body trembled, the organ tones swelled.

"Do I not frighten . . .?" he declared bitterly, continuing to watch the mirror, his face silently staring as if mocking him. "Better were it had nature given me a mind consistent with my outer self. Could I not have lived in ignorant bliss . . .?"

His hands shifted to the manual of the great organ. The swelling measures of the "Prize Song" rose to its magnificent climax. The room reverberated.

"A loathsome creature, despised . . . unloved . . . condemned. Condemned to live," he soliloquized. "My mind, my studies, my futile appreciation of the arts . . . wasted in a meaningless, hostile world. A life of useless quest and frustration. Why could it not have been otherwise . . .? Have I not had to take by violence that which is rightfully mine? Alone, I shall achieve that which You have so maliciously taken from me!" So he bitterly indicted his Maker.

The music changed to the softer strains of the lyric theme. Again, he looked up into the mirror.

"Oh, Cynthia!" he went on, murmuring to himself. "You, the fruit of my knowledge . . . the work of my hand. Did I not take you from death? Had it not been for my timely rescue, you would be rotting in your grave . . . a sickening specter of shrunken flesh and bones, a plaything for worms."

Through the doorway between the parted curtains came the black-velvet clad figure of Cynthia. In the purplish glow, which accentuated her strong features and lent a ghastly hue to her ashen face, she moved in the soft spot of light like an automaton of wax. Her somber eyes looking straight ahead, her gown trailing luxuriously, she moved across the richly carpeted room toward a full-length mirror. With a start, as if suddenly awakened from a deep trance, she turned quickly in front of the mirror and glared across to Schalkenbach.

"The music! The music!" she burst out in a shrill high-pitched voice, stopping her ears. "I cannot stand it! I could scream!"

The Wagnerian strains stopped. He rose from the organ bench. Rearing like a gorilla, he ambled down the altar-like steps of the dais and crossed the room to her.

"Why do you persist in tormenting me?" she demanded, her eyes dilating. "You know the playing of the pipe organ tears at my nerves. It is as if the rumble of a thousand drums were madly beating in my ears. I simply cannot bear it—it destroys—" She faltered and then broke off sharply.

Dr. Schalkenbach gazed down upon her, bewildered, "But the music should intoxicate—the beautiful melody, it should uplift you—inspire you," he explained, making an awkward gesture with his massive hands. "I had hoped that you would respond."

"Look for yourself, what you have made of me!" she cried out impatiently, glaring into the mirror, her pallid face taut and sunken, her eyes glowing within their deep sockets. "Will there be no end . . .?"

Dr. Schalkenbach stepped back.

"I shall overcome that," he declared, as Cynthia drew her slender fingers hopelessly over her deathly face "You must be patient.

"Then, give me back myself—restore my beauty," she implored. Your promises . . . what are your promises?"

"Ah!" he exclaimed triumphantly. "But you have vanity—that is something. Soon," he added firmly, "you will have everlasting beauty."

"Are you not going to stop this?" she cried harshly. "Why must I become this creature?" She paused and lowered her voice. "I do not understand. I want to live—to feel. Yet, somehow, I cannot. I am strange and cold. I—"

"Perhaps it is only yourself you love," he interrupted in a loud tone. "Like Narcissus, you care ouly for your own image. Vanity will destroy you."

"Destroy me?" she retorted, a metallic ring in her voice. You have—" She broke off sharply.

"Cynthia, you must believe in me," he went on, his voice firm. "You must have faith. Soon you shall blossom in all your, sweetness like an enchanted song—a symbol of the morning glory. You will understand the beauty of the red rose, the color of the sea's faint purple mist." His eyes lit up. "We will go far away," he whispered in eager warmth, "perhaps to the mountains . . . to the pine-scented slopes where gurgling brooks and cascading streams How . . . to a spring that is placid and cold . . . where the dazzling sun will give us warmth and a new life. All nature will blend in a gay, sylvan symphony. There, *mein Liebchen*, we will find—happiness."

Cynthia breathed wheezily.

"But that is impossible—the sun I loathe!" she drawled bitterly. "I . . . don't want—" Her voice faltered and broke off in a hoarse gasp.

"I will overcome everything. You shall be a paragon," he boasted pompously, "the symbol of the ultimate, the embodiment of an ideal." His eyes blazed wildly. "I shall not be dubbed a botcher," he roared, pounding his chest. "They won't laugh at Schalkenbach!" He paused, his expression changed. "You shall be the woman who lived again," he whispered tenderly.

Clad in a mandarin robe and wearing loose slippers, Ying Tsung silently slithered into the room. Confronting Dr. Schalkenbach with his yellow-hued, enigmatic face, he made a half-bow and stood erect. His coal-black, slanted, eyes narrowed sinisterly into a slit. He mumbled briefly in Cantonese. Dr. Schalkenbach nodded sullenly. Then complacently, the Oriental turned, glided away, and disappeared behind the billowing draperies.

Cynthia shook convulsively. Her breathing labored, came in short rasping gasps. Wan and suddenly emaciated, she was like some unearthly creature, sibilant and cadaverous. Dr. Schalkenbach took her by the arm and he led her, panting and shaking, in the direction Ying Tsung had taken. The weird sound of her voice trailed off behind the curtains.

The lights dimmed into a faint glow. The muffled clink of a steel door shutting sounded. Then a man's terrified scream issued from the passageway back of the draperies. It was a fearsome cry of horror, which rose to a high pitch and died as if it had been smothered behind the closing of doors.

~§~

In the laboratory, its labyrinth of stone-slabbed tables jumbled with chemicals, goose-necked flasks, burettes, and steaming retorts, stood the bulky mass of Dr. Schalkenbach, robed in a surgeon's white gown. Bathed in a spotlight of purple, he held up a fuming test tube before the glowing Rontgen globe suspended above his head. On the table beside him was an array of large cylindrical glass tubes sealed by spiral electrodes. A green phosphorescence vapor sputtered and hissed as it played up and down in the glass.

Looking down upon him, its bulldog face wrinkled in a sneer, its fanglike teeth protruding and its wings spread wide, was the huge body of a mounted bat. In the corner, visible between two of the glowing cylinders, reposed a human skeleton, its skull fixed in a grimace. Through a darkened door at the side of the laboratory appeared Ying Tsung. He slithered across the chamber to Dr. Schalkenbach.

"I am prepared to go!" he announced, clipping his words.

Engrossed in his examination of the test tube before the purplish light, the doctor nodded absently. "Ten pounds of chloroform," he said without turning from his work. "If it is too late, try the chemist's."

Expressionless, the Oriental shook his head and departed.

Dr. Schalkenbach set the test tube in a rack, picked up a large hypodermic syringe, wiped it in a swab of cotton and inserted its long needle into the test tube. Then carefully eying the graduation marks on the instrument, he drew off accurately a portion of the milky, effervescent solution. With the syringe in his hand he lumbered across the laboratory to an operating table, where the slender figure of Cynthia lay motionless in the black velvet gown under the purplish rays of a vapor lamp. Her cheeks were full and slightly flushed. She peered languidly up at him. Bending down over the table, he kissed her lightly on the forehead. Then, pushing up the sleeve of her gown, he gently pressed the hypodermic needle into her slender arm.

"This is something new! It's a glandular secretion—ductless gland I've prepared from a living person," he announced with a slight touch of grandiloquence. "It may prove the turning point in my experiment." He straightened and looked thoughtful. "The ductless glands of the body," he went on, impressively, "are in reality the seat of the human soul. These glands are balanced in their harmonious secretions which condition the human behavior, and the functions of the intellect. If I'm successful in duplicating synthetically the secretions of these glands I could at will produce a genius, saint or devil, or any condition that marks the erratic scale of human behavior."

Cynthia's large, somber eyes stared half-credulously up at him.

"Then, I must go out tonight?" she inquired in a slow,

guttural voice.

"How do you feel?"

"As always afterwards. Drowsy and full, as if I'd never care to have another drop."

"Your complexion, your eyes, are better than I've seen them before," he said with quiet elation. "But I must send you out tonight—once more." He sat down heavily on a stool and leaned over her. "Perhaps in a day you will have reached a crisis," he added slowly. "A few more treatments and we'll taper off."

His rugged bulk hanging over her fragile beauty, his primitive features accentuated by his bulging eyes and long bushy lashes, made an incongruous picture of a monstrous cave man zealously watching over his strange beauteous prize.

Silently he pondered as his eyes gazed enraptured upon her loveliness. He was lonely. He felt now that she was more beautiful, more radiant than ever before. To him she was a symbol of love and life—a flower soon to blossom forth in fragrance and glory. The hot blood flamed in his cheeks, burning with sweet fear and joy that made him long for her yet shrink with horror from even the thought of the possible consequences. He recalled the days when they first met. They were days of rapture. He had never before known the kindness, the inspiration, the warmth of woman. Now but a sweet memory, a will-o'-the-wisp, gone with time. Would he triumph over this barrier to earthly happiness? His black eyes glowing with tender emotion, he rose slowly. Bending over the table, he gently slipped his hand under her shoulders, drawing her body close into the warm folds of his large arms. He trembled, his thick sensuous lips quivered. His ardent love was crying out for expression, but the cold, lifeless response of her body hanging limply in his embrace checked the burning passion surging within him. He lowered his cheek to hers. She was icy, responseless. She lay emotionless in his arms, as silent and placid as if she were a wax mannequin.

"It is of no use," he murmured at length, releasing her from his clasp. He shook, his head slowly, hopelessly.

"I cannot be a brute."

He stood abstractly for a moment, staring at the racks of chemicals and simmering flasks. Then he turned heavily and ambled across the laboratory to the scrubbing basins. Washing his hands, he looked up at the reflection of himself in the oblong mirror. He stared bitterly at his image. He slowly fingered over his nodular flesh. He twisted his blubber lips. He bared his wide irregular teeth.

"Beauty is not physical. Beauty is something felt— something understood," he declared, continuing to gaze into the glass. "Does not my face belie me?" He made a weird grimace.

His bulging black eyes glared mockingly back at him. He drew his fingers through his bushy hair, which fell in disorder about his distorted features.

A grin broke across his face as he saw in fancy the reflected image of his inner self. In the mirror a handsome strong countenance appeared, a face with smooth, ruddy complexion and dark vivid eyes that set off his black well-groomed hair and fine aquiline nose. About his firm lips played a proud smile.

"The charming Dr. Eric von Schalkenbach," he acknowledged with significant emphasis, bowing complacently to himself. "The charming—" He broke off sharply, grinned incredulously at the image—then burst into a sardonic laugh.

"Alas! It's only me! Me . . . myself—myself talking to myself!" He laughed bitterly again.

A small translucent screen on the side of the laboratory wall lighted. Dr. Schalkenbach looked up, startled. It flashed again . . . a third time . . . and a fourth.

"That's strange," he muttered, grimly. "Ying Tsung back already."

He slipped off his surgeon's gown and in his lumbering gait hastened from the laboratory, and wound his way up a spiral iron stairway. Reaching the dimly lighted hall, he stopped before the beam of the electric eyes and peered out through a telescopic sight at the side of the steel door. In the optical frame of the instrument he saw an elderly woman in a black cape and bonnet standing in the vestibule. Her arms were concealed under the cape which bulged noticeably on the right side. The doctor straightened, ran his fingers along the seam of the door jamb, pressed a button. The thick armor plate slowly rose, disappearing into the ceiling. A quaint Colonial door stood revealed. He backed himself close to the side of the wall and swung it open. The woman stepped in from the vestibule. The steel plate slowly descended, clinked shut.

"Well—what is it?" Dr. Schalkenbach demanded.

"I come back early," declared Ying Tsung, pulling off the bonnet and gray wig. "I bring important news."

From under his cloak he brought out a batch of newspapers. Quickly Dr. Schalkenbach seized them and eagerly he scanned the glaring headlines staring him in the face.

Blared the *Post*:

BAT WOMAN PANICS CITY
BLOODLESS VICTIMS FOUND

Screamed the *Telegram*:

KENT JAIMSON GRID STAR
BLOOD MURDER VICTIM

Shouted the *Journal*:

BLOOD-LAPPING VAMPIRE
SLAUGHTERS THREE

Proclaimed the *Sun*:

KENT JAIMSON MURDERED
VOODOO FIEND VICTIM

He read, "Police seek a monsterous man, Dr. Schalkenbach . . . "

The papers crackled and crumpled in the tightening vicelike grip of his massive fist. His eyes blazed savagely.

"So . . . So they would meddle—would they?" he said

in slow deliberation. *"Die verfluchten Schweine . . . !"* He Hung his hairy arms up over his head and waved them furiously.

15

As she sat in the group in easy chairs around a crackling log fire, with the butler serving after-dinner coffee, her Nordic fairness, accentuated by a dinner gown of vivid blue, Katherine Van Allen turned to Colonel Hadlow Winthrop.

"I simply must get to town tomorrow," she said. "I've a luncheon at the St. Regis and so many things I must do."

"We'll have to see about that, young lady," the Colonel replied gravely. "Remember there is danger, and you are too precious for us to lose".

Katherine's teeth flashed in the firelight. "So, I'm the poor little bird in the cage, am I?"

"I'm sure it would be quite all right to go in during the day," Robert put in. "I'll drop you, and perhaps you'll have time to meet me at Louis'. He makes a swell Sazerac!"

"I'd like to if you won't mind packages. I may have some, and I know a girl with a lot of them is one of your pet aversions."

"I won't mind them too much if you carry them!"

The Colonel, sipping his coffee, leaned forward and set the cup on the tray.

"If the Sazeracs are as good as they are in New Orleans," he remarked, with the trace of a smile, "I won't expect either of you back. But I do wish you would both return before dark."

Katherine smiled brightly across to Robert. "In spite of your dislike of packages, young fellow, I'd like to bring out my skis. Can you pick me up at the house?"

Robert laughed.

"Is that all?" he answered dubiously. "If I get them, you'll have to promise to go skiing—and no reneging, either."

The butler opened the door. "Professor Huxford is here, sir," he announced, stepping aside. The Colonel and Robert rose. The criminologist strode into the drawing-room. Smiling, he nodded to Katherine.

"Your guard at the gate is extremely efficient." He chuckled as he shook hands with the Colonel. "I almost didn't get in. I suppose that's my punishment for making the suggestion."

"Why didn't you phone us? I would have sent the car for you."

"I appreciate that, but I was detained and hardly knew what train I could make. Between the newshawks and the Academy of Medicine, I've been kept on the run. Evading pertinent questions, of course."

"I trust you're staying overnight with us?" the Colonel inquired, as Robert drew up a chair for him.

"I'd like to very much," he replied. "The operator at my apartment tells me my phone has been, ringing incessantly. The reporters are keeping close on my heels, but I'm sure I can find peace out here."

"Why don't you stay for the weekend?" the Colonel urged. "You'll find it restful, and you can have the use of a car at any time."

"Thanks, I should enjoy staying. The Manor is very beautiful. It's hard to realize we are so near the city."

"I believe you'd like it even better in the summer. I hope you can visit us later, when the trees are in bloom and the yachting season is in full swing. We're old salts and spend much time on my yawl."

Robert offered cigarettes.

"Katherine is quite surprised at the newspapers," he said, holding a light for her. "Perhaps she is more amused."

Katherine's turquoise-blue eyes sparkled. "Yes, the papers have simply dramatized this horrible affair to the limit," she said in her slow, throaty voice. "You'd think the whole of New York was in danger."

Huxford nodded. "The story has crowded the war news right off the front page." He smiled. "I can imagine the embarrassment of Dr. Schalkenbach. I trust, Miss Van Allen, you haven't been upset by my suggested precaution?"

"Oh, no, not in the least. But I do feel uneasy about Robert. I hope he won't be foolish enough to go hunting for trouble again."

"He's a very lucky young man. And I must compliment him on his coolness. The information he has contributed is very valuable. I'm sure it'll be of assistance in tracking down this mad Doctor."

"What are the police going to do?" Robert asked.

"They've planted a squad of plain-clothes men in the Washington Square vicinity. Before leaving I was in touch with Inspector Hogan. He says his men are in the neighborhood, but as yet with no results. I venture to say Dr. Schalkenbach's lieutenant, the Chinese, is using a disguise. However, by noon tomorrow we expect to have information that will close us in on our objective."

"Then, I suppose, they'll rush in with all the fireworks," the Colonel remarked. "I hope they don't make another two-gun Crowley circus out of it."

"Hardly!" Huxford smiled faintly. "I've suggested to Inspector Hogan that his undercover men act with the utmost precaution. With Dr. Schalkenbach and his colleague Ying Tsung now informed by the newspapers, they will of course be on the lookout for any suspicious persons loitering in the neighborhood. Therefore, any false move would most certainly tip off Schalkenbach. If this should happen before we can put our finger on his hideout, he might attempt to destroy all incriminating evidence. On the other hand, Dr. Schalkenbach, with his selfish unbalanced ego complex, his unrelenting determination to complete his inhuman experiment, and thinking himself secure within a virtual fort, may have the conceit to defy the law.

"You must also bear in mind that up until this moment the police haven't a tangible thing against him in fact, not even sufficient circumstantial evidence to get an indictment. Barring, of course, Robert's testimony and the rather delicate Cynthia Winthrop angle."

"Then what are we going to do about Cynthia?" Robert broke in. "We can't let her go on that way."

"You'll have to leave that to me personally," Huxford replied gravely. "It's an extremely difficult situation— indeed, unique."

"Of course, you know," the Colonel put in, "that Mr. Jaimson stated to the press that his son was with Rohert the night he disappeared. Are you sure, Dr. Huxford," he added with apparent unconcern, "that nothing has got out that will link the name of Winthrop with the case?"

"No direct link. A hawk-eyed reporter did insinuate perhaps I should say broached the question. But I believe he was just sending out a feeler. You know I have Inspector Hogan pretty much in my hand." Huxford smiled slyly. "I'm sure he won't be so indiscreet as to take any step without first consulting me. I believe I hold the trumps in this game."

"An Associated Press man phoned here this after-noon," said Robert. "He wanted to know what I had to say about the murder of Kent. I told him I knew nothing, that he was a close friend, and that I was greatly shocked by his death."

"Dad also got an inquiry," added Katherine. "He told them I'd gone away for the weekend. They were very per-sistent—wanted me to pose in a bathing-suit. Dad's a great teaser, and he finally shooed them away with a handful of horrible old pictures of me looking like a ghastly chromo that he got out of Aunt Maybell's album."

"They must have the attractive girl in the case," Huxford remarked with a twinkle. "She adds what the newspaper boys call 'the legs'."

The Colonel slowly stroked his Vandyke and looked at Huxford inquiringly.

"I presume, Doctor, your visit to the Academy of Medicine proved profitable," he said.

"Yes, quite," Huxford answered. "There were several angles to this case which puzzled me. I'm indeed thankful now that I went. What I found at least cleared a matter in my mind which may have done a grave injustice to an innocent party."

"You mean you have the solution to Cynthia's strange death?" asked Robert quickly.

"Precisely," Huxford stated. "I was especially interested in my search of the archives to find a case of human vampirism and its scientific relation to the bat; that is, to *Desmodus rufus*, the bloodsucking hat. I found not only a treatise on bats, but a most extraordinary chronicle of a Russian surgeon who lived in the nineteenth century. According to the brief diary found among his effects, he had conducted a unique experiment in vampirism with a wolfhound. They were good enough to lend me a copy of this amazing paper and also a popular book on bats, which I've brought along in my briefcase."

Huxford paused, his eyes narrowed slightly. "I feel I should at once clear Dr. Judd of any suspicion. In view of all the facts I've gathered I'm convinced that his diagnosis of African sleeping sickness, which he withheld from the death certificate, was the incorrect one for Cynthia Winthrop's so-called strange malady. It was, as the death certificate says, the type of sleeping sickness known to this continent," he stated emphatically. "Her death, if I may term it that, was brought about not by the bite of the teste fly, the African parasite-carrier, but by the 'little surgeon'—*Desmodus rufus*."

Huxford paused to take a cigarette and light it.

"This bloodsucking mammal, a menace in the Tropics," he continued, settling back in his chair and languidly blowing a stream of smoke, "has been proved to be a carrier of the sleeping trypansome disease and paralytic rabies—fatal to animals and sometimes to man. The bat in this case was no doubt imported from South America. A part of Dr. Schalkenbach's ruthless and cruel scheme to get the woman he wanted. There's no question in my mind that on his return from the Tropics he deliberately stole out here under cover of darkness and planted an infected 'little surgeon' in Mrs. Winthrop's bedroom. Her trancelike sleep and the deep unconsciousness which followed, and so perplexed Dr. Judd, was the result of the infection caused after the thirsty bat had drawn its quota of blood."

"Oh! how perfectly revolting!" Katherine said, her voice quivering. "I'd die if one got in my room. Why didn't the horrible thing awaken her?"

"It would not wake anyone. The vampire bat is indeed a quiet worker. Moreover, because of its razorlike teeth, the victim seldom realizes he has been bitten till light reveals the stains of blood. The creature is extremely dexterous. It rears up on its legs and walks, having short but strong hind legs. It can stalk easily, using its wings as 'thumbs.' And it guzzles blood with its long tongue like a cat lapping a bowl of milk. When these bats are starved for blood, they become furious fighters, and have been known to attack in gangs both man and beast, with sanguinary violence."

"Is it not true a bat can whiff a person to sleep?" asked Robert.

"With the cold, stupefying breath of its wings?" asked Huxford. "Well, there's a certain superstition that a vampire bat hovers over its victim and fans them into deep unconsciousness with its black leather wings. In the tropics, there are peasants who stoutly maintain that they've had this experience. I can't vouch for the truth of this belief," —his eyes twinkled— "but I might read you a letter written by an old Trinidadian whom Raymond Ditmars and William Bridges quote in their book *Snake-Hunter's Holiday*."

He took a book from his briefcase and quickly thumbed its pages. "Here's the letter!" he said. Then leaning slightly forward he began to read:

"Having to accept a night's lodging in a cacao house of an old peasant proprietor in the Cutucupano Valley, Santa Cruz, and to share a portion of the drying floor with the hospitable old man, and being minus of any but the clothes

I slept in, my thoughtful host provided me with an empty cacao bag which he said would be necessary for me to get into, as the 'surgeon'—meaning the bloodsucking bat-would be sure to operate on my great toe if precautions were not taken to cover them snugly.

"Being thus forewarned, I got into the bag and pulled it up neatly to the armpits and buckled my elastic band belt over to keep the enemy away from my feet. It was not long before I heard the flutter of the wings of a bat, as it flew along the length of the floor, and the voice of my host saying, 'Look out! The surgeon has arrived.' I made a determined effort to keep awake, in the hope of catching the animal if and when it made a descent upon me.

"Things became quiet and all I could see was the weak glow of a small lamp at the far end of the floor. Taking no chances, I decided to keep awake and await events. The evening was close and warm, and a deathlike stillness prevailed when I heard another flutter of wings, the creature coming toward me, this time passing slowly within a foot of my face, leaving a sensation of cool, wafted air.

"'Aha!' I thought, 'you will soon venture too near and I will seize you with my hands as soon as you touch me.' The process was repeated once, twice, in close succession, the sensation growing more and more soothing, and a drowsy feeling began to creep over me, which completely overcame me after the last fanning, and I fell into a heavy sleep, until I was awakened by a smart, burning pain in the tip of the great toe several hours after I had fallen asleep.

"Feeling something crawling up my leg, I tried to seize

it, but I failed to do so and it escaped through the loose end of the bag, which, during the night, had become unfastened through the slipping of the belt.

"The wound, which was oval in shape and neatly cutout, bled profusely and was too painful to the touch to bear the pressure of a shoe until I placed my foot in the cool water of a running stream for about three hours."

~§~

Colonel Winthrop's eyes brightened.

"I heard the same sort of yam told in Africa," he stated. "There may be some truth in it, though personally I never had an encounter with the 'little surgeon'—*Desmodus rufus.*"

"But, Dr. Huxford," Robert asked eagerly, "how did Schalkenbach manage to get bold of Cynthia? We all saw her after Dr. Judd had pronounced her dead."

"It's quite evident that the woman you saw dead was not your wife, but one substituted by Dr. Schalkenbach. The very fact that the exhumation disclosed an unidentified body which bore an exceptionally marked resemblance to your wife convinces me of that. In fact, your family dentist, Dr. Zell, was amazed at the close likeness. It was not until he had consulted her dental chart that he had any idea that the body was not hers."

"Then you believe that she was taken from her bedroom?" asked Robert.

"Yes. My reason for believing so is primarily the fact

that embalming would have made her utterly useless for the purpose of his experiment. It would be entirely possible for him to come out here, climb the balcony to the second floor, bide his time, and enter her bedroom. For a giant who can subdue an enormous crocodile with the ease that Captain Sheldon described to us, it would be a simple matter to carry a woman on one arm, scale the walls, substitute her for Mrs. Winthrop, and carry the latter away.

"It would not be a difficult task for Dr. Schalkenbach, with his fiendish practice of using human beings for his experiments, to acquire a young woman who resembled your wife. Her emaciated condition, following her protracted coma, made it easy for him to make the substitution without arousing suspicion. The woman Dr. Judd pronounced dead was not Cynthia Winthrop. The fact she had changed so much during the course of her illness, coupled with the fact that no one had any reason for suspicion, would make it unlikely that the exchange would be noticed. It would be all the easier for Dr. Schalkenbach because he undoubtedly possesses plastic skill in molding the human form and could make the victim conform to Mrs. Winthrop's emaciated state."

"Do you believe she was alive when abducted?" questioned the Colonel.

"You'll recall I was told that your son's wife supposedly died while the night nurse was downstairs having her lunch. She stated she'd been gone about thirty minutes.

Well, it was undoubtedly during this time that Schalkenbach made the substitution. Of course, he changed her night clothes and attended to the other details with meticulous care.

"I shouldn't want to say positively whether she was dead or alive when she was removed. But from what I've learned about the conditions of his experiment, I'd venture to say that she died after her abduction. The very fact that she's no longer a normal person indicates that she had died and then been restored to the helpless creature she now is.

"As I recall, Dr. Judd stated that the body was perceptibly warm when he arrived, and fixed the time of death at about 1:30 A.M. This would indicate that the woman Dr. Schalkenbach brought here for the substitution must have been still alive but dying when he entered Mrs. Winthrop's bedroom."

"But can you explain the strange form of life of what was once Cynthia?" asked Robert quietly.

"That is a point I intended going into," Huxford replied.

"The paper I obtained from the Academy of Medicine this afternoon will, I believe, throw considerable light on Dr. Schalkenbach's experiment in vampirism. It's the only document on the subject I could find after an exhaustive search. It gives an authentic case taken from the annals of the medical society," he explained, taking from his briefcase a yellowed pamphlet patched with adhesive tape.

"This paper was published in 1872," he went on, "and chronicles the extraordinary experiment in biology of a Russian surgeon, one Dr. Serge Crususviski. Before I read you his diary, which I hope will make clear my reasoning, I shall attempt to outline an incident in the bizarre life of this doctor which involved him in a rather embarrassing situation with the law and led to his somewhat hurried flight to South America." Huxford glanced at the paper. "As a fugitive from justice, he lived obscurely in a cabin in the jungle hills on the outskirts of Guayaquil, Ecuador. After his death two years later, a diary was found among his effects, in an impoverished laboratory. . .

"To get back to the incident which led to his flight from Odessa and across the Black Sea to Istanbul, this Dr. Crususviski, according to the editor's note, had a mad obsession. He contended that the brain could be made to survive after dissociation from the body. Of course, he was scoffed at by his colleagues, which infuriated the Russian and made him all the more desirous to prove his theory.

"I shall spare you the horror of the account, which is printed here in all its gory detail. It seems that he had a beautiful wife, and that he conducted his experiments in a basement laboratory in his own home. In order to prove his theory and impress his fellow scientists, he invited them to his laboratory to witness a demonstration. With dubious smiles the gray-haired savants filed into a makeshift amphitheater. In the center stood a metal table, on which rested a boxlike screen. Under the table were jars with thermometers connected to rubber tubes, and a compressor. The tubes pulsated with the rhythmic beat of the pump. One of the jars was immersed in a warm bath heated by a crude oil lamp. Dr. Crususviski, clad impressively in a surgeon's spotless white gown, appeared before them. He addressed them:

"Gentlemen, I have invited you to witness for the first time the proof of my theory. I have managed by an exceedingly delicate operation to preserve successfully a severed brain and its nerve center for a period of twelve hours. This has been made possible by the regulated circulation of blood to the arteries connecting the brain—what I term an artificial heart."

"With a flourish he withdrew the opaque screen, disclosing the lovely blonde head of his wife. A gasp of horror escaped the group as they stared at the living head, which rested on a large platter connected with the apparatus. The bright eyes wandered curiously about the astonished group. Then complacently the mad surgeon picked up a strip of raw meat. Gloating at his fellow savants, with sadistic pleasure he dangled the bit of food before the quivering red lips of his wife's severed head, which opened as if trying to swallow the morsel.

Huxford relaxed in his chair. "Needless to say," he remarked dryly, "a charge of murder was immediately brought against the Doctor. But as I've already said, he escaped before the authorities could apprehend him. The next time he was heard of was two years later at Guayaquil, Ecuador, where his diary was found. It was in this document that I discovered information which has particular bearing on the case of Cynthia Winthrop." He turned the yellowed pages of the journal carefully. "Here's the brief record of the doctor's singular experiment in vampirism.

It's a translation from the Russian, and the diary begins in the year 1873. I will begin to read at the date June 3. Santa is his wolfhound."

~§~

"Living alone in the hills of Guayaquil, I have resolved to carry on my work the best I can. Out of a few instruments and chemicals the near-by pueblo provides and with the contributions of my friend the German assayer, I have fashioned in my cabin a crude but serviceable laboratory. From earthen jars made by the Indians, silver ingots, and zinc from the mines, I constructed a series of galvanic batteries.

"I had intended performing my experiment on a live llama, but today I noticed that Santa was languid. The country is infested with a ferocious bat which appears at night and preys on animals. Last night one got into my cabin, attracted by the light. I caught it alive by knocking it to the floor with a blanket. This morning I have examined the creature. I find that this fanged type of mammal thrives on blood. Santa was bitten by one of these bats. I suspect his stupor was brought about by its lance-like nip.

"June 4. My wolfhound refused all nourishment. His eyes have taken on a wild look. By prying open his mouth with the utmost patience, I have managed to force food into his system.

"June 5. Early this morning I went with the net and sack to a cave in a neaby pass, where I had previously noted bats hanging in great numbers in the dark caverns. With little effort, I captured sixteen of this bloodsucking species. Not wishing to be burdened with more, I returned to my cabin and placed them in a dark enclosure. Tonight, I allowed them to feast on a llama. I peeped through a small hole and observed that the bats gouged their fangs into the animal until glutted, when they dropped off.

"June 6. The llama appeared little the worse for its donation of blood. Determined to find out whether the bite is the cure, I cautiously removed a full-glutted bat, and with a large syringe and needle drew off about ten cubic centimeters of warm blood from its storage sac. Immediately thereupon I injected this into the jugular vein of Santa. Tonight, I allowed the bats to feast again on the llama.

"June 8. This morning my wolfhound showed improvement. I gave him another injection. Went down into the pueblo and got supplies from the almacen. Saw my friend Karl, the assayer. He gave me a sack of ammonia crystals.

"June 9. I wetted down the crystals in my galvanic cells. This afternoon I connected them with strands of copper. When I brought the copper joints together I got a hot spark. I am overjoyed at this. I believe I am the first man in these parts to accomplish this. Santa has lost the gain he made yesterday. Tried again to force food. Was obliged to give blood injections in its place.

"June 10. Awakened at daylight by Santa scratching at my door. He had evidently been out all night, having jumped out of an open kitchen window. This is the first time the animal has done this. Gave another blood injection. These transfusions from the bat are entirely taking the place of food.

"June 12. Santa had a relapse today. The blood injections seem to have lost their beneficial effects. Before I retired to my room I was obliged to lock Santa up. He has become slightly distempered.

"June 13. Spent most of day working with galvanic cells and my silver needle, one of the few things I brought from Odessa. Karl came over this evening. He brought me a galvanometer, which he had constructed at the assay office. I am afraid I shall lose my friend. He talks about returning to Germany.

"June 14. It has rained incessantly since last night. Unable to get supplies. Santa lapsed into a coma. Gave him two blood transfusions. Refilled my water barrels.

"June 15. Santa lapsed into deep unconsciousness and died. I connected my silver needle with the galvanic cells and inserted it into the wolfhound's heart, penetrating the right auricle. I regulated the current and sent fifteen volts through the animal's heart, gradually decreasing the voltage. After some minutes, my stethoscope showed Santa's heart to be faintly pulsating. This afternoon Santa feebly got up. I am disquieted to note a wild look in the dog's eyes. He does not recognize me.

"June 16. Before daylight I fed a fresh llama to the bats. Santa pants and snarls when in want of blood. Gave him two injections. He refuses any other form of nourishment.

"June 19. Have increased the transfusions. Santa subsists entirely on blood injections. Tried again to wean him from this form of diet. He completely ignored food placed before him. I noted tonight that his eyes glowed with a peculiar green phosphorescence. Becoming uneasy about this, I bolted my door before retiring.

"June 22. Still trying to wean Santa from the injecttions. I put a saucer of warm blood taken direct from the llama before Santa. He ravishingly lapped the entire contents.

"June 23. Santa continues to lap blood. Have tried giving solid food, but without success. I have stopped the injections altogether. Santa is now contented to subsist entirely on lapping fresh blood. Terrific electrical storm shook the cabin tonight, followed by torrential rain. Santa bayed continuously during the storm. He growled and snapped at me so violently that I had to chain him up in a dark closet.

"June 24. Santa quieted before daylight and fell into his usual daytime state of lethargy. When I opened the closet door he snarled, his eyes glaring at me savagely. After sunset, he crawled out and lapped up two liters of fresh blood. He feasted copiously, then bounded out of the door. I called but he paid no attention. He disappeared down the dark canyon trail.

"June 25. Santa returned just before daylight. He ignored a fresh bowl of blood I put out for him, and went snarling into his dark closet."

~§~

Huxford concluded, and looked up.

"This was Dr. Serge Crususviski's last entry," he said, relaxing in his chair. "However, there's an editorial note which goes on to explain that as the Russian's friend, the assayer, had not seen him for several days, he climbed the trail to his cabin. He found the door wide open and the surgeon's effects scattered about the place. In the bunk room, he was shocked to see the doctor, fully dressed, sprawled on the floor, with a frozen look of horror on his face."

"What had happened?" Robert broke in.

"Well, according to the assayer's statement," Huxford answered, "it looked as if the Russian fugitive had been furiously attacked by a beast with jagged fangs—his throat had been ripped to pieces. A fact that perplexed the examining authorities no end was the surprising one that they found about the mutilated body practically not a drop of blood. With the permission of the police the saddened assayer gathered the scattered pages of his friend's diary and on his return to Germany, he took the recordings with him and told the following story:"

"It was several weeks after the Russian's violent death that an English prospector, with his Indian helper and laden pack animals, set out from his mountain cabin toward the distant pueblo of Guayaquil.

Impeded by their llama pack train, which was burdened with heavy canvas bags of high-grade, and the
ruggedness of the winding trails, some kilometers from
the pueblo the two miners were overtaken by darkness.
Not having experienced the luxuries of civilization for
some months and eager to spend the night amid the
gaiety of the pueblo, the zealous Englishman and his
wiry henchman got in the rear of their pack train and
drove the bleating animals before them.

"Suddenly from on top a jagged boulder at some
height above the trail there appeared a pair of fire-like
eyes. The animal snarled at them, showing protruding
fangs. Hastily and with practiced precision, the cool
Englishman slung his carbine to his shoulder and fired
at the ghostly head. Unaffected by the shot, the animal
pounced down upon him so quickly that the agile
Indian barely had time to escape. The growling of the
infuriated beast mingled with his master's dying
groans so terrified the man that he abandoned his
partner and fled from the canyon.

"Reaching the pueblo, running and shouting, the
Indian alarmed its languid inhabitants, and breath-
lessly told the astonished natives of the beastly assault.
Later, the authorities reported that the body of the
unfortunate English prospector was found to have
been savagely gouged about the throat and, like that of
the Russian fugitive, it was bloodless."

Huxford concluded, leaned forward, slid the pamphlet
into his briefcase. An oppressive silence fell over the group.
Katherine raised her long lashes and looked wanly across
at Robert, who opened a pack of cigarettes, grimly offered

them, took one, tapped a smoke on the packet, and put the box back in his side pocket.

At length Colonel Winthrop's voice broke the stillness. "Then, Dr. Huxford," he said slowly, "you believe there's a parallel between Dr. Crususviski's experiment and that of Dr. Schalkenbach?"

"Unquestionably! This Russian scientist was more than half a century ahead of his time." He paused and slowly shook his head. "It's too bad his energies were so horribly misdirected."

"So, you believe that Dr. Schalkenbach brought Cynthia back to life?" Robert asked tensely.

"Yes. Reviewing her case history and in the light of Dr. Crususviski's experiment, I'm convinced that Cynthia Winthrop died shortly after her abduction, and was restored to a form of life by an improved model of the Russian's 'heart-starter'."

"It may be of interest to know that only recently a group of scientists perfected an electrical instrument which in several cases has actually started the heart of persons dead as long as twelve minutes. This instrument is merely a refinement of the Russian doctor's electric needle. The heart has a natural pacemaker in the right auricle, consisting of a group of cells that develop on an electric current of about one-thousandth of a volt. This current from the auricle spreads through the heart and causes its muscles to contract periodically. The needle which is inserted in the muscle supplies the initial impulse which starts the heart action. The fact that Cynthia

Winthrop has become what we might term a living corpse is sufficient proof that she must have died and been revived."

"What stage of vampirism do you believe she's reached?" the Colonel asked.

"I've no hesitation in saying that, judging from the two bodies I examined at the Morgue, she is only in the early stages. In fact, it would appear that Dr. Schalkenbach is doing everything in his power to make her normal. The last stages of vampirism are not unlike cannibalism," he continued with quiet authority. "A person who becomes habituated to drinking blood in time becomes entirely dependent upon it, even attacking others to get sustenance.

"I recall the case of a shipwrecked sailor who for a protracted period survived on the flesh of his shipmates. The habit became so ingrained in the man that later he resorted to the most brutal murders in order to satisfy his cannibalistic taste. When he was apprehended, he astounded the authorities by telling them that human flesh was the only diet on which he had subsisted for almost a year. He remarked that he preferred people who did not smoke, as the flesh of the chronic tobacco-users was bitter and not to his epicurean taste. He turned to Robert, his eyes twinkling. "So young man," he said, "should you ever find yourself shipwrecked on a cannibal island be nonchalant and light a cigarette."

Robert straightened in his chair and grinned sheepishly. "What happened, then, when the blond fellow was forced into the glass compartment?" he asked soberly.

"And those terrifying cries?"

"The rows of compartments which you were so curious about house his vampire bats. Judging by the countless marks of their sharp teeth which I discovered on the bodies of the two victims I have seen, I should estimate that he has at least several hundred of these bloodsucking terrors. And from your description. I should say that the victim is led into one of the chambers of starved bats, which drop *en masse* upon the helpless person and feast like gigantic leeches upon his blood until they become satiated.

"It's not a pleasant subject to bring up," Huxford added in an apologetic toile, "but I believe Dr. Schalkenbach is transfusing the blood of vampire bats taken from their victims into Cynthia's blood—a method not unlike that which Dr. Crususviski employed in his experiment with his wolfhound—"

The Colonel interrupted. "How do you account for Dr. Schalkenbach's getting into the country with this cargo of infernal bats? I don't see how he could have entered in the ordinary way without attracting a great deal of attention."

"I doubt very much that he's in the country legally. Most probably after Dr. Hampden was put off the schooner at the port of Surabaya in Java, Dr. Schalkenbach, master of the *Swift Star*, sailed across the Pacific and landed in some obscure spot along the California coast. The heavy boxes contained his wealth and the chests with perforations housed his vampire bats. I'm convinced that the strapping Kaffir sailor who Dr. Hampden says disappeared under rather strange circumstances, and who Dr. Schalkenbach claimed had died suddenly, was sacrificed to the bats."

"Katherine interrupted. "Please!" she exclaimed in a pained voice, turning her clean-cut face toward Huxford and smiling pitifully, "I'll be dreaming about these horrible things if you don't stop."

The Colonel smiled at her. "Young lady, when once this awful affair is over, and you and Robert get on your skis in the good sun, you'll forget soon enough. Perhaps it's just as well."

"Then how about a good stiff nightcap?" suggested Robert, rising to his feet.

"Not a bad idea," Huxford agreed.

"I'd like an Alexander," said Katherine.

"You can make mine a two-finger Scotch highball," put in Huxford.

"I'll stick to my rye and soda, Robert," added the Colonel, getting up and walking over to the Gothic bay window.

"It's a good night to be indoors," he remarked, peering out over the snow-mantled grounds and the expanse of the bleak Sound. "The visibility is exceptionally good. Execution Light is quite bright tonight." He turned to Huxford. "Your room, Doctor, is right in its path. I trust its flashing won't keep you awake?"

"Not at all," the criminologist replied. "After the blinking neon signs and the din of the city's frightful night traffic it would take more than the swinging beam of a mere lighthouse to disturb my slumber. Sometimes I think

I shall quit New York forever."

Robert entered the drawing-room, gingerly balancing a laden tray.

"I hope I haven't made these too potent," he remarked, setting the drinks down on a low table.

"After hearing such gory tales, one needs a very strong drink," declared Katherine, taking her cocktail from the tray.

The Colonel raised his glass, and toasted:

"To all wholesome things!"

16

THE night was bleak and cold. A man in an ulster with its wide-winged collar upturned, his mittened hands clapping from time to time, slowly patrolled the long sea wall in front of the rambling Winthrop mansion. In the distance, the powerful revolving beam from the lighthouse swung through the darkness, momentarily silhouetting the barren trees against the spotlighted house, sweeping past the rugged shore line, and vanishing off across the expanse of water. A light mist, drifting in from the Sound, was slowly enveloping the peninsula, thinly veiling the dock and the boathouse, and turning the channel lights into glowing specks.

The bright yellow moon emerged from behind a sullen black cloud, bathing the somber Gothic dwelling, its upper front windows lighted, in its pale beams. A window suddenly became dark. In an adjacent room that opened with French doors onto an ornate balcony a watcher might have seen the figure of a girl in negligee. From the Sound came the muffled chugging of a boat. Its dim running lights slowly passed, floating in the mist like the eyes of a specter.

At the entrance to the snow-covered grounds a husky figure lounged about the gate. A snow-rutted road leading from the estate merged in the distance with the white landscape. And beyond in the mist appeared and disappeared the occasional lights of a moving vehicle. A car swung abruptly into the road. Its headlights glaring before it, the machine approached the gate. The guard peered at the car's dark outline. It stopped, backed away, turned, and disappeared down the road, its tall light fading in the distance.

Inside the mansion there was the silence of dead sleep. The place was in darkness except for a green lamp. In the foyer and a single light glowing dimly in Katherine Van Allen's room. Throng the French doors which opened from her room onto the balcony streamed the pallid moonbeams, softly lighting the low bed and setting off her long fair hair, which fell over her pillow in a wealth of silken gold.

A pale-blue silk dressing-gown had been carelessly thrown across the bed. On a nightstand stood a vase of long-stemmed roses, and beside the flowers lay a closed book. The room was silent save for the monotonous lapping of the water against the rocky shore line and the distant drone of an airplane, sounds which entered through the partly opened French doors.

Of a sudden the creeping shadow of a hand appeared on the wall at the head of Katherine's bed. Imperceptibly, it grew into the semblance of a long arm. The beam from the lighthouse turned through the room and vanished. The shadow withdrew, and then reappeared. The hand reached out, its long talonlike fingers sinisterly spread out as if to clutch something. Slowly the shape of a head and shoulders was thrown grotesquely over the entire wall. The shadow swayed over the sleeping figure like a huge gorilla, its hairy arms gradually descending upon her relaxed body. Outside the French doors, and hatless, his arms embracing the doors like an octopus, stood the rugged bulk of Dr. Schalkenbach. He pressed his nose against one of the glass panels and peered avidly into the chamber. Then stealthily, he reached out and around the door and inch by inch edged it open. Like a reared bear swaying from side to side, his long arms and massive hands swinging like heavy pendulums, he ambled noiselessly into the room and toward the bed. Bending his huge body over the sleeping figure, he put out his hairy hands and lightly touched the blanket covering her as if to turn it back. Startled, he straightened, cocked his head, listened. The beam from Execution Light slowly passed through the room.

Katherine shifted restlessly in her sleep. Again, he bent down over her, again his arms stealthily went out. Her eyes opened. She blinked. He became motionless as her eyes widened in horror. A long piercing scream burst the stillness of the night. Deftly he slipped his arm under her waist. In one single, dexterous movement as if he were executing the artistry of an adagio dance, he swept her out of bed. Hastily he threw the blue negligee about her.

Katherine's face went white, and then her lithe figure swung limply from his side. Her blond hair streamed below in a profusion of gold. The dainty negligee clinging to her lovely body setting off the fresh whiteness of her skin and revealing her firm, slow-curving breast, Schalkenbach lumbered with her toward the doors.

As he reached the balcony, the beam from the light-house flashed. For an instant, his hulking form and his inert burden was highlighted, making a bizarre picture like a fantastic tableau of beauty and the beast. The patter of footsteps sounded running in the hall; doors opened; lights flashed on. In a dressing-robe, high-powered rifle in hand, the Colonel reached Katherine's room. Huxford slightly disheveled, arrived at his side.

"Did you hear her scream?" the Colonel asked. Huxford nodded. "Yes, we'd better enter."

The Colonel rapped excitedly, hesitated, then flung the door open. They rushed into the bedroom and through the wide-open doors onto the balcony.

"She's not here! Huxford exclaimed. "Can you see any-thing?"

"Yes, there he goes with her!" pointed out the Colonel, raising his gun. Breaking through the snow in a bounding gait, the huge bulk of Dr. Schalkenbach receded in the distance. Colonel Winthrop lowered his gun and started for the door.

Huxford seized the Colonel's arm.

"Wait!" he said. "It's too late for that. He already has her in a fast car. The police must be notified at once. I'll have them send out a radio alarm." He hurried from the room, followed by the Colonel.

In the hall, Huxford lifted a phone, jiggled the instrument. He jiggled it again, impatiently. There was no response.

"The line's dead," he said tersely. "Schalkenbach didn't overlook a thing."

"What's happened?" shouted Robert in the hall, trying to get into his bathrobe. "What was that scream? I thought I was hearing things."

"You did! Katherine's gone. Schalkenbach's got her!" the Colonel retorted, grimly.

"What!" replied Robert, dumfounded. "Gone—?"

In a tassled cap and baggy nightgown the butler suddenly appeared at the foot of the stairs. "My word," the ludicrous looking man proclaimed in a loud indignant tone, "I never saw the likes of it!"

"Get dressed quick!" called Huxford as he ran toward his bedroom. The Colonel and his son obeyed the order, and in less than four minutes all three dashed back in the hall. The cook and maids were milling around the butler, chattering and gesticulating.

"I see everyone but the chauffeur," said the Colonel hastily, scowling as he glanced down at the scanty clad, excited servants. Robert, you will have to drive us. I hope you'll find a key in one of the cars."

"Better meet us at the gate, Winthrop," said Huxford to Robert, groping with his unbuttoned collar. "We'll be waiting there." Young Winthrop nodded abruptly and turned off down the hall to a rear stairway and entrance.

Huxford and the Colonel took the steps two at a time, reached the foyer, passed the amazed servants, slipped on their overcoats, snatched their hats, and rushed out the front door. They went over the stone stoop in a skip and headed down the drive toward the gate. Brandishing a large pistol, a bleareyed guard came running up from the back of the Manor and joined them.

"What's up, Chief—anything I can do?"

"Yes, you may put that thing in your hand away and quit pointing it at me," Huxford ordered. "You're too late to use it."

"I heard nothin'!" the guard stammered.

"Where's your partner?" demanded the Colonel, turning up the collar of his overcoat.

"He's watchin' the gate, sir."

"Why, the gate's wide open!" the Colonel declared, as they went down the drive. "But I don't see him."

They reached the tall wrought-iron structure. The large padlock had been sprung clean out its case and the heavy chains were on the ground. Huxford examined them.

"Hum!" he muttered. "Looks as if a terrific pressure had been suddenly brought against the gate, not unlike a battering ram. I wonder where the guard is?"

"Here are fresh footprints!" the Colonel broke in, pointing out in the moonlight a trampled spot from which a track led away through the snow parallel to the high wall. "Looks as if there's been a struggle."

"Yes," observed Huxford quickly, as he picked up the trail and followed it accompanied by the Colonel and the guard. "They're exceptionally far apart for a normal stride. The deep imprint angle and the distance between the right and left foot indicate that they were made by a man bearing a heavy weight on his right side."

Huxford stopped short. The group halted behind him. The path of footprints forked, one branch going off in the direction of the house, the other, with a returning track, toward the wall, where under a tree a dark object lay.

Huxford turned to the guard.

"Let me have your light," he ordered. The man whipped out a cylindrical flashlight and flipped it to him. Huxford shot the beam of light under the tree. He advanced then abruptly stopped and played the light on a sprawled figure. "Here's your missing guard," he announced soberly, bending down and tearing the man's shirt open. He made a hasty examination.

"Any bullet wounds?" the Colonel inquired.

"No. Not a sign of blood. He must have been so quickly attacked that he didn't have a chance."

"*Jessss . . . us!*" moaned the guard, gaping at the prone body of his partner. "Not even a break to pull his rod!"

"Yes, that's right—not even a chance," Huxford said, shaking his head. "Looks as if his neck was snapped. Done so quickly he didn't know what happened." The headlights of an automobile in the direction of the house were seen. Its glaring lights swept the group, went down the drive, and came to a stop at the gate. The blatant noise of its horn sounded.

"Robert's waiting," the Colonel said hastily. "He'll go mad if he doesn't know where we are."

"There's nothing we can do here. This man is dead," Huxford stated. "We've lost too much time already." Without further delay the Colonel and Huxford left the guard and hurried to the gate where young Winthrop sat behind the wheel of a station wagon.

"Larchmont Police! Step on it!" the Colonel shouted, climbing into the back of the machine as Huxford tumbled in.

The wagon lurched and shot through the gateway, speeded down the narrow road. Turning and careening through the winding streets of the quiet village, they reached the Post Road and came to a stop in front of the trim suburban police quarters. Huxford strode up to the Sergeant's desk.

"There's been a murder and kidnapping on the Point."

"Not at your place, Colonel Winthrop?" interrupted the dazed Sergeant, turning to the Colonel, his eyes popping.

"Yes, I'm afraid so," he replied, frowning.

Robert sank into a chair in a corner, lighted a cigarette nervously.

"I'm working with Inspector Hogan," went on Huxford.

"I want to use your phone."

"O.K.!" snapped the Sergeant, picking up the instrument, "Spring 7-3100," he ordered into the mouth. The Colonel nodded to Huxford, stepped to the side of the desk and slipped out into the corridor. The Sergeant handed over the phone to the criminologist.

"Homicide Bureau," said Huxford imperatively to the police operator. Huxford talking from Larchmont," he explained, rapidly speaking to the brisk voice at the other end. "Yes, Rex Huxford, I'm calling on the Schalkenbach case—" He broke off, listened. "Yes, that's right," he repeated. Schalkenbach case—description in your files. Twenty minutes ago, he broke into the Winthrop estate at Larchmont, killed a guard, and kidnapped Katherine Van Allen of New York. Suggest you order radio alarm. Watch all approaches, especially from the north and the east. Probably. heading for New York in car with girl of medium height, blond hair, blue eyes. Age twenty-three, weight 130 pounds. Notify the undercover detail to be on lookout in Precinct Six. Leave message for Inspector Hogan to call my office in morning." He hung up.

"I'll get two men right over, Professor," the Sergeant said with awe. "I'll get the Chief." He barked an order at two of his men, who were lolling outside the door of his office.

~§~

Back at the Winthrop house in the living room, with the log fire now smoldering, the Colonel mixed a Scotch and soda from a portable service bar beside his lounging chair. He passed it to Huxford and poured one for himself. Robert paced the room.

"What are we going to do?" he cried, stopping his pacing for the moment. "What are we going to say to her father?"

Huxford calmly sipped his drink.

"It won't do any good to get excited," he said. "The chances are that it would have happened just the same in town."

"I've already informed Mr. Van Allen," interrupted the Colonel, putting his empty glass on the portable bar. "I telephoned while you, Doctor, were talking to the Sergeant. I tried to make it plain that everything humanly possible is being done."

Robert turned to Huxford.

"Why do you think Schalkenbach wanted her?" he demanded.

Huxford frowned.

"It's quite obvious he's struck back on account of our interference," he replied. "We can blame the Medical Examiner and the newspapers. I was afraid of this all along. He may have the audacity to use her as a hostage—the price of getting us off the case. On the other hand, there's no telling what he may do with her.

"There's one thing certain," he went on in a firm tone. "Regardless of the consequences, we shall get him. Dr.

Schalkenbach has definitely compromised himself. He's played right into the hands of the law and is now vulnerable. With casts of his footprints, the evidence of the slain guard, and the fact that he has abducted Miss Van Allen, justifies drastic action. Perhaps a raid on his hideout."

"I'm afraid tonight's developments are going to put us in a most embarrassing situation," the Colonel remarked gravely, as he poured himself another Scotch and soda. "They're apt to bring to light the rather delicate matter we've been trying to suppress."

"I don't agree with you," Huxford replied quietly.

"With the morning papers shouting the story of the kidnapping, the police concentrating on the capture of Dr. Schalkenbach, and Inspector Hogan depending on me for feathering his cap—there'll be little to fear on that score. The newshawks, however, I'm quite certain, will be most curious to know why you had guards on duty here. That's a detail that I'm sure you can explain. Better just frankly tell them you feared violence because of your son's close friendship with Kent Jaimson. There's a chance, of course, that Schalkenbach may be picked up before daylight."

"That reminds me," the Colonel said, "I've neglected to notify the telephone company that our line is out of order."

Huxford smiled wryly. "It may be just as well. You might need a switchboard before many hours."

The distant ringing of a bell sounded.

"That's the front door—I'd better take care of it,"

Robert said, stopping his pacing and hurrying from the room.

"I suggest we try to get a few hours' sleep," said the Colonel.

"Yes," agreed Huxford. "I must get to the office early."

A chubby-faced policeman, holding his cap in his hand, entered the room with Robert.

"Sorry to bother you, Colonel," apologized the patrolman, standing erect in his heavy uniform coat. "The Chief thought he'd better put two men at your gate. Beats hell how word goes travelin'. People are already out there. The Medical Examiner—he just left."

Huxford broke in. "What did he find?"

"Sir, his neck and back was busted. The Doc's all puzzled. Said he don't see how it could have happened. The black-wagon just took the body."

"Well," said the Colonel, "if your men get a little weary, tell them my butler will fix them up."

"Thank you, sir! We'll take you up on that." The patrolman grinned, turning to go.

After the door had shut out the figure of the patrolman Huxford turned to the Colonel and remarked:

"Back-snapping seems to be a religion with Schalkenbach. You'll remember that Dr. Hampden said his henchman, Ying Tsung, boasted that he prides himself on never using a weapon."

"He's a fiend, a ruthless killer!" exploded Robert, raging and pacing the room. "He's robbed me of my wife— made her the inhuman, tortured creature she is. He's murdered Kent, my best friend. Now he's taken Katherine from me—and we sit here like a lot of old women as if nothing had happened. Why don't we do something?"

17

EMERGING from the lower level of the Grand Central Station with the morning crowd of rushing commuters, Huxford, swinging his Malacca cane, strode out onto Forty-Second Street.

In front of the wide-arched entrance the shrill clamor of newsboys assailed his ears. They were shouting and yelling: "*Extra! Extra!* All about the big kidnapping! *Extra!* Seek maniac in vampire snatch! Voodoo fiend kidnaps society beauty! *Extra! Extra!* Girl in negligee cave man victim! Police mobilize in man hunt! *Extra . . . !*" Speedy trucks laden with papers joggled into the curb; eager news vendors pounced upon plopped bundles; jostling crowds demanded papers; newsboys screamed: "*Extra! Extra!* Grid star murderer adds another victim! Famous sleuth outwitted! *Extra . . . !*" Tabloids glared full-page scare lines. Huxford flipped a coin to a boy, grabbed a paper, and got into a taxi. A grim smile played about the corner of his mouth as a paragraph lead caught his eye: "GLAMOROUS DEB SNATCHED FROM BED WHILE FAMOUS SLEUTH SLEEPS." The cab turned from the curb and sped away.

At Rockefeller Center, Huxford stepped out of the elevator on the sixtieth floor, turned the wide corridor, and found a crowd overflowing from his office into the hall. As he strode up, the milling assemblage quieted and crowded around him. Then questions were fired at him like pellets from a machine gun.

"Are you working for the Winthrops?"

"Is it true a ransom note was received?"

"In't it true the Van Allen girl was slugged?"

"I'll give you a statement later," he countered, pushing his way through the persistent throng, followed by the glum-faced Inspector Hogan.

"Holy hell's poppin'!" snorted the Inspector, shutting the door behind him and plumping down on the edge of Huxford's desk.

"And I suppose you think I don't know it?" rejoined Huxford, seating himself in his swivel chair. "Apparently the papers are trying to put the blast on me, as the boys say." He chuckled.

"You know more about this case than you're spilling," ventured the Inspector, shoving his Fedora back on his forehead. "But don't get me wrong, Governor—I'm playing ball with you."

Huxford nodded, his eyes brightened. "That's quite true, Hogan. But I'm not holding out anything that will retard you in closing the case."

"O.K., Boss. I'm keeping my trap shut, ain't I?" Huxford nodded. The Inspector straightened his hat. "The Commissioner put me on the spot this morning," he went on. "Ordered me in no uncertain terms to clean this case up—bring in this fellow Schalkenbach today, and no mistake. He didn't say bow. But be gave me the whole undercover squad to bust this."

"We'll have to work fast, Hogan," said Huxford emphatically. "The Van Allen girl will be in danger if we don't get to his hideout at once. What have your men reported?"

"After the Department got your message every approach was covered. I don't think he coulda slipped through our net. He may be layin' low outside. Two men were picked up in the Village. They were hangin' around Washington Square about three o'clock this morning. One was a Filipino. My man who brought him in thought he might be that Chink, Ying Tsung. The other fellow's a parolee—done a stretch up the river for burglary."

"I don't believe you'll find either of them connected with the case," said Huxford dryly. "I'm pretty certain our man is working only with his lieutenant, Ying Tsung."

"Our best bet fell flat," the Inspector went on. "A clerk at Elko, that East Side chemical firm, said he remembered the Chink. Said he had bought quantities of chemicals and apparatus during the past year. Paid cash and took everything with him. But he didn't know his name or where he lived. We also got a report on a limousine drawing up along Waverly Place at four o'clock this morning. Some people got out and hurried into one of them houses. Before my man could get there, it had gone."

"Was he certain of the house?"

"Yeah. He's sure it's one of three houses. He didn't go

any farther—said they were all dark."

"Did anyone of them have a high stoop?" Huxford asked, his eyes narrowing.

"Yeah. I asked my man. The whole row of them houses are alike."

"Hum", commented Huxford. "Any other developments?"

"Nothing much yet. On your tip, we're still runnin' down them house leases. We've got twenty-two more to check. My men are also makin' quiet inquiries. So far we haven't got a thing on 'em. Five families are away—accordin' to the neighbors, none of them people answer to the description of this Schalkenbach or that Chink." The Inspector drew out a cigar, bit off its end and spat it on the floor. "By the way, Professor!" he asked condescendingly. "What did them boy scouts in Larchmont find? Suppose they got the case sewed tight."

"The boys are right on the job," Huxford assured him. You've got to hand it to them. They've accumulated enough evidence to convict Dr. Schalkenbach—a good cast of his footprints and excellent fingerprints from the French door."

"Did he bump off that guard the way the papers say?"

"The account I read, I thought, was exceptionally accurate. You know, it's a characteristic of this Dr. Schalkenbach to kill without a weapon."

"Can we bank on that?"

"So far as I know."

"Then you don't think his hideout's an arsenal?"

"I don't believe you'll find him so crude. He's a scientist, and too astute a strategist for that sort of thing. However, don't let that mislead you. I'm quite sure he won't be so polite as to invite us into his parlor for cookies."

"Huh!" grunted the Inspector. "Tough guy—aha . . . ?"

Huxford's secretary entered hesitantly.

"The reporters want you to answer these questions," she explained, handing over some yellow sheets of paper. "They want a statement for the noon editions."

He nodded. "Just a minute," he said, taking a pencil in hand. "I'll answer them now." He wrote rapidly. "I'm not handing out too much."

"Right!" said the Inspector. "Them fellows gum the works. They know more than we do."

Huxford returned the sheets to his secretary. "You might tell them I haven't answered all their questions, but Inspector Hogan may have an important announcement to make later." He tilted back and turned to the Inspector.

"I take it Hogan, you have a man covering those brownstones on Waverly Place?"

"Yeah. I got two plants down there."

"Then what have you found out? Did you get any report from them on the tenants?"

"Sure. There's six houses in that block facing the square. They're all four stories and owned by wealthy people. The tenants in three are away and the places boarded up tight as a clam. One of the joints is occupied by old Lulu Markham and her sister, Eliza. The family's old-timers—been livin' there since Fulton steamer up the river.

Old Lulu is lousy with dough."

"Yes, I've heard of the family," said Huxford. "The father was a pioneer in the cloak and suit industry. He made his money in bustles."

A light flashed on Huxford's desk. He picked up the phone. "Yes," he answered. "Send him right in." He turned to the inspector. "A man from the Federal Bureau of Investigation outside. I wonder what he wants."

A wiry man of about thirty-five in loosely fitting tweeds, a light gabardine coat slung over his arm, entered the office briskly. Huxford rose. "Glad to know you, Mr. Carruthers. This is Inspector Hogan of the Homicide Bureau. He is with me on the Van Allen case."

Inspector Hogan nodded, with a wave of his chubby hand.

"I've come to get a report on the Van Allen kidnapping," the government man said. "I've just interviewed Mr. Van Allen."

"What are you fellows doing on this?" barked Hogan. "This ain't a case for you G-men."

"I'm not quite so sure of that, Inspector," he answered coolly. "Mr. Van Allen just received a message from the abductor demanding that the Winthrops drop the investigation at once or he'll find his daughter dead. This Dr. Schalkenbach may have taken her over a state line—to New Jersey, for example. Incidentally, Professor Huxford, your name was mentioned."

"Have you got the message?" demanded the Inspector.

"No," replied the government man. "It was given over

the phone."

"I suppose you fellows already got the lines tapped grumbled the Inspector.

"I'm sorry, Inspector Hogan," Carruthers replied in an ironical tone. "We haven't as yet any reason to enter the case, but we may have, and we like to be in our cases early."

The Inspector bit savagely down on his cigar.

"Huh," he grunted, "we ain't gonna let up! I've got my orders to stay put. And put we gonna stay," he added emphatically.

"That's not for us to say," was the suave reply. "So far our hands are tied. We have no proof that he has crossed the state line."

"I'm fairly sure that he hasn't, Mr. Carruthers," said Huxford. "I'm afraid we'll be obliged to stall. But you are wise to find out what you can." He paused, then went on: "It'll be necessary to tell Mr. Van Allen and inform the press that we will withdraw providing she is released at once. That will give us more time to work under cover. I'm convinced that her safety demands that we push forward unrelentingly with our plans; but we are justified in the deception. It would be senseless to give this mad egoists quarter."

"We received information this morning on Dr. Schalkenbach," said the government man. "He's illegally in this country. The State Department records show that he entered the United States and later cleared for Pará, Brazil."

Huxford smiled. "You fellows haven't been asleep,

have you?"

"It's nothing at all." Carruthers shrugged deprecatingly. "We have a complete report from Germany in our
files." He rose. "Don't hesitate, Professor, to call upon us if
you need help. And good luck," he added briefly, nodding.

The Inspector's shrewd steel-blue eyes followed the
government man out of the office.

"Our Department don't want any o' them G-men chis-
elin' in," he remarked bitterly. "Last time them guys pulled
a fast one. Busted in with the artillery—hogged the show
before we had a Chink's chance."

Huxford abruptly rose from behind his desk.

"Well, Inspector, let's get going," he announced. I'd
like to take a look at those brownstones in the Village."

"O.K., Governor," Hogan agreed, slipping his weight
from the desk to the floor. "My men are downstairs in the
car."

When Inspector Hogan and Huxford came out
through the revolving door onto Rockefeller Plaza a black
streamlined sedan moved up to the canopy. The Inspector
opened the door and they climbed into the back.

"Washington Square, and go down Fifth Avenue!" he
ordered a swarthy, clean-shaven man behind the wheel.

The car shot away from the curb, turned the corner,
and sped down the avenue. A bull-necked man with a
military haircut who was sitting beside the driver reached
over the back. "I guess we won't need this baby—yet," he
said, pulling up a tommy gun and edging it into the recess
back of his seat.

As the sedan approached Eighth Street the Inspector leaned forward and spoke to the driver. "Ease her over to the curb and wait. The Professor wants to take a look at the layout." He turned to Huxford and added, "While we're here I'd like to drop in on them Markham dames and hear what they got to say."

"A splendid idea," Huxford agreed, getting out of the car, followed by the stocky form of the Inspector.

As they walked west on Waverly Place, Hogan's gimlet eyes squinting from under his pulled-down Fedora, Huxford breezily swinging his Malacca cane, the two men accurately took in the row of dull brick houses.

"Here's the Markham place," the Inspector mumbled. "They all look alike and got them green shutters. A hell of a place for a guy to find when he comes home on a bender."

"They most certainly are alike," Huxford agreed, as they ascended the stone steps of the third house. "And the way they have their blinds shut you'd think they were afraid of sunlight."

"Most o' the tenants are away," remarked Hogan, searching the vestibule for the bell. "I told you that."

Huxford smiled. "I don't think you'll find a bell, Inspector. But there's a perfectly good knocker staring you in the face."

"Cripes!" The Inspector raised the bright polished hammer and rapped.

A wizened, hawk-eyed man in black opened the door a little and peered out at them suspiciously.

"Whom do you wish to see?" the man demanded in a

nasal tone. The Inspector flashed his department badge before the man's eyes, which opened wide at the sight.

"Oh, the police!" he exclaimed, indignantly.

"Yeah!" snapped the Inspector. "You tell Miss Markham that Professor Huxford and Inspector Hogan want to see her. Understand!"

"Er—er—yes gentlemen. Step . . . step right in, gentlemen," the man faltered, standing a little to one side and holding the door open. "Er—be seated in the parlor. I . . . will announce you."

In the dimly lighted, high-ceilinged room with its gilded antique furniture and dismal oil portraits of black-mustached men, the Inspector solemnly removed his Fedora and gingerly sat down on a fragile silk-covered chair.

Huxford chose a more substantial chair.

"Huh—!" muttered Hogan, glancing around at his surroundings.

"They say the old dame won't even have a phone in the joint."

Huxford nodded. "It's like stepping into a bit of the gay nineties," he remarked, observing a gaslight chandelier of shimmering glass crystals. "The period certainly has been religiously kept intact."

"Yeah, get a load of that china closet with them curios and that bedpan—"

Swishing silk and the patter of descending feet sounded in the hall. An aristocratic old lady in a mid-Victorian black silk dress with bell sleeves entered the room. Huxford rose.

"We're very sorry to intrude, Miss Markham," he explained. "We wish to make some inquiries about your neighbors."

"Miss Eliza, my sister, and I have been living here since we were children," she answered in a high-pitched, cultivated voice "but nowadays we hardly know our neighbors. I hope nothing disgraceful has happened?"

"Nothin' yet, Miss Markham," stated the Inspector. "We want to know about the folks in the second house down."

"The only family we're acquainted with are the Hewetts. The Commander, you know, died last year, and since then his children have closed the place and are galivanting around Europe. Young people these days don't care to stay at home."

"Did you or your sister ever see the occupants of the house on the other side of the Hewetts?" questioned Huxford.

"I can't be certain of that," she replied after a moment's hesitation. "The occupants of that house are exceptionally quiet. We have never heard of any complaints."

"Have you ever seen the tenants?"

"My sister and I sit a great deal at the widow looking over the square, and I don't remember seeing them," she replied. "But last autumn we saw a middle-aged woman come out on several occasions. That is all we know."

"At any particular time?"

"Yes, it was always in the evening, about nine o'clock.

I especially remember the time because it was shortly be-fore the hour at which we retire."

"Have you ever heard any unusual sounds near here?"

"Oh, nothing that I'd call exactly unusual," she an-swered in a precise tone. "We have sometimes heard the distant rumbling of an organ late at night. If that's what you mean? My sister and I are very fond of music, and we have often wondered where it was coming from."

Huxford's eyes narrowed to a slit.

"Can't you give us some idea where the sound came from?" he asked.

She looked thoughtful.

"It sounded as if it might have come from Commander Hewett's house. But I know," she added positively, "that they have no organ."

"Thank you very much, Miss Markham," Huxford said, rising to go. "We may find it necessary to speak to you again."

The bilious-looking butler held the door open, peering curiously from behind it as he slowly closed it after them, his popping eyes following them out through the vestibule and down the stoop.

The Inspector straightened his Fedora.

"Well, it looks like we're smack up a blind alley," he grumbled to Huxford as they reached the sidewalk. "The old dame don't know what it's all about, livin' there in the dark like a shut-in with all that dough."

"On the contrary," Huxford said quickly, "despite her age she has a pretty keen sense of hearing. Perhaps it would interest you to know, Inspector," he added dryly, his eyes brightening, "that our friend Dr. Schalkenbach is also a musician. He probably has a pipe organ in his quarters."

"Wh—what—?" stammered the Inspector, stopping in his tracks. "I'll pull my men in and close in on this block."

"Not so fast, Hogan," Huxford cautioned. "We might first consider the place Miss Markham said the woman came out of. I doubt whether she could hear an organ from the house on the comer. There are too many thick walls between the two places."

"I've got every house in this row accounted for except the comer and that Number 217," stated the Inspector.

"The one the dame came out of."

"Well," said Huxford casually, swinging his cane in the direction of a four-story brick house with drawn shutters. "This 217 looks like our best bet. I think it would be a good idea to take a chance and see who lives there."

"O. K., Governor, it's your show," he quickly agreed, and then beckoned with a nod to a thin man in a black overcoat who was approaching them.

The man, carrying a package under his arm and his hat pulled down shading his eyes, stopped as he reached them.

Inspector Hogan turned to the man. "Get this, Sergeant," he ordered in a low voice. "We are ringin' bells. Understand? Might go in 217. I want a plant outside. If we're not out in fifteen minutes, order the squad in. Understand?"

The plain-clothes man nodded, and continued on his

way. The Inspector and Huxford strolled to the front of Number 217 and turned up the stone steps of the house next to the boarded-up Hewett house.

"Should they ask questions here, we'll say we're inquiring about the caretaker of the Hewett place," Huxford murmured.

The Inspector shook his head, and opened the vestibule door. They, stepped into a well-kept enclosure. A large white Colonial door confronted them.

"Cripes, these joints are all alike. They haven't even a honest-to-God bell," the Inspector declared as he searched the sides of the door. "Governor" he instructed the criminologist, "you'd better give that knocker a couple o' jabs."

Huxford hooked his Malacca cane on his arm and brought the hammer down with sharp metallic thuds. He grinned.

"Perhaps we'll be invited in for afternoon tea."

Stern-faced, the Inspector snaked his service .45 from its armpit holster and buried the gun in his overcoat pocket. He motioned Huxford to stand to the side.

After a short interval of waiting Huxford leaned out and again raised the knocker, rapping more insistently. Tensely they held their breath listened.

"Huh!" grunted the Inspector at length "Funny no one comes" He pulled from his pocket a bunch of keys. "I'll try my passkey."

He jiggled the key in the lock, turned the knob cautiously and then flung the door open."

"I'll be God-damned . . . ! he said, drawing back. An

armor-plate door . . . !"

Huxford nodded with grim satisfaction.

"Yes, a fortress!"

18

HUXFORD sat at his desk looking contemplatively out over the city, its lights beginning to twinkle in vast orderly patterns, the sunset back-lighting with a reddish glow the towering buildings and the rich-hued horizon. He tilted back in his swivel chair and slowly drew on his lighted cigarette.

"I'm glad you dropped in. I was thinking of calling you at Larchmont," he said across the desk to Robert, who sat stiffly eyeing him questioningly, his pale face tense.

"I hope Katherine is in no immediate danger," Robert declared anxiously. "Are you positive he doesn't suspect?"

"I hardly believe he does," Huxford replied. "He's not apt to be up to anything at once. At least while he's holding her as a hostage and demanding that we quit the investigation. Inspector Hogan is of the opinion that he may be hiding outside the city. I'm convinced, though, that he brought Katherine to Washington Square early this morning. He was probably asleep when we were at his door."

"Then you and the police propose to go right ahead regardless of Mr. Van Allen's request?" Robert questioned, his voice slightly raised. "Father agrees with him and has withdrawn."

"Yes, I know," Huxford replied calmly. "If we hadn't found his quarters this afternoon, I might also have been willing to withdraw. But it's too late now to turn back. Regardless of Dr. Schalkenbach's demands or promises, we're going right ahead."

"Are the police going to raid his place at once?" asked Robert tensely.

Huxford nodded. "I'm waiting now for Inspector Hogan," he answered. "The house is surrounded by plain-clothes men. But before the Inspector orders his men in, he wants to be certain that Dr. Schalkenbach and his accomplices are bottled up."

"You are sure this move won't be bad for Katherine?"

"How can it be? The men will move rapidly. There will be no time for Dr. Schalkenbach to do anything but try to escape."

"Then, what are we going to do about Cynthia . . . ?"

Huxford frowned and shifted restlessly in his chair.

"I'm afraid that's going to be our most difficult problem," he replied grimly. "I don't like to think what might become of her—or what we'll have to do. You must realize that this is a matter the existing law is incapable of dealing with. Our problem is not unlike that of a mercy killing."

"Just—just what have you in mind?" faltered Robert.

Huxford's eyes narrowed.

"I'm glad you're here," he said. "I wanted to talk this over with you. It may be necessary to take the matter in our own hands. If we should, it will require drastic action—"

He broke off sharply, leaned forward, drew open a side desk drawer, and took out a .45 caliber automatic pistol.

Robert's eyes widened as they caught sight of the gun and followed the weapon into the criminologist's armpit holster.

"I understand," he gasped, turning deathly white. Now that we're about to face the grim reality, I can realize the horror of our gruesome—"

The signal light on the desk flashed. Huxford reached for the phone. "Yes. Send him in," he said crisply. He replaced the instrument.

In a dark overcoat bulging at its sides, Inspector Hogan stepped into the office and closed the door behind him.

"Everything's set, Governor!" he announced looking Robert over quizzically.

Huxford rose from behind the desk. "Inspector Hogan, I'd like you to meet young Mr. Winthrop."

The Inspector's steel-blue eyes glinted.

"That's a tough break you got kid. Well," he snorted, "it won't be long now. We're gonna plant that wise gorilla flat behind the eight ball. We'll mow him down like nothin'!"

Huxford stepped to a corner in the room.

"How about Mr. Winthrop coming along?" he suggested, taking his coat from the rack and slipping into it. I may want him to help me."

"Sure, what the hell—pack the kid along!" Turning to Robert, he grinned. "Think you can stomach it . . .?"

"I'll take the chance."

"I suppose the reporters got tipped off?" Huxford said to the Inspector as they strode from the office down the corridor. "They've been hot on my trail all afternoon."

"Yeah, they're all wised up." He shrugged. "Well, it won't amount to a good damn, now."

They came out onto Rockefeller Plaza and the Inspector led the way across the wide sidewalk to a sedan waiting near the canopied entrance. A second car parked close behind was packed with the black figures of men sitting stiffy, their hats pulled down to shade their faces. Stepping up to the first car, the Inspector opened the door and the three men got in.

"Get going!" he ordered the man behind the wheel. Trailed by the second sedan, the car shot away from the curb, turned down into the evening Fifth Avenue traffic, it's jumble of dancing lights giving way before the shrieking sirens of the two speeding police cars. The glimmering city lights blinked past, sharp blasting whistles rent the air, as the two onrushing machines wove their way screaming past red lights. Cars drew abruptly to the side, taxi drivers swore, jammed brakes moaned, and pedestrians gaped.

~§~

Dr. Schalkenbach's massive bulk, robed in white, stood towering in his laboratory before his table of assorted surgical instruments, filtrates, and fuming test tubes. The chamber was still except for the monotonous thump of boiling water, an occasional muffled squeak like the chatter of mice, and the purr of hissing steam which issued from a seething retort.

He picked up the large hypodermic syringe, carefully wiped its long needle with a swab of cotton, and placed it in a porcelain cabinet. Bending down over the slab-bed table, with a flick of his finger he turned off the flame under the boiling retort. Straightening, he slipped out of his surgeon's gown and lumbered across to the operating table, where Cynthia lay in her velvet gown.

Like a giant sentinel he stood silently over her, his bulging eyes fixed in fascination upon her loveliness.

Slowly she stirred. Her black eyes looked up glowing with a sparkling tenderness he had never before seen in them. Vaguely, as in the fleeting moments of a dream her past was parading before her as she lay trancelike, gazing up at the man who had taken her from death. Though she had never given herself to him, now she felt a strange confusion of warmth and fear for the man who had made her his own. Like a wandering soul she was dimly conscious of a remote past, desolate and long lost, now triumping over a dark barrier that had so inexplicably separated her from it, and verging once more with the present into earthly happiness. Slowly she rose, as though still heavy and confused with sleep. His blubber lips tightened as he eyed her in wonderment. She looked at him strangely. Then, as if she were awaking from a profound sleep, remembrance came with a rush, and she swooned into his arms.

Exultation swept over him as his eyes flashed triumphantly at her fragile body folded in his embrace. With almost womanly tenderness he soothed her, holding her still in his arms. Swinging her gently in the cradle of his embrace, he rose from under the purplish glow. Her slender arms encircled him, he drew her close to his body. Her lips touched his softly.

"It's over," he said at length. "Over and finished. It's a new life we've begun together a new life that will bring you warmth and strength. We will go away, far away, to breathe the bright morning sun of life. Forever," he murmured, his voice trailing off into a whisper as he carried her from the laboratory, "forever and forever . . . "

In the darkened music room, he lowered her slowly till her feet touched the floor. Through the parted curtains opening into the adjoining room, the stately canopied bed was partly revealed. Soft light streamed over them, casting long shadows on the walls.

A bitter sob escaped her.

"I've been so terrible—so utterly horrible," she said with quivering lips. "Forgive me . . . ?"

"There's nothing to forgive, *mein Liebchen*," he replied gently, his voice fading as he lowered his head close against the soft velvet shielding her breast. "A life—a newborn life is ours."

Vaguely she felt him take her once more in his arm. and hold her crushed against his massive body. A pleasing warmth stole over her. And dimly in her ears, as if nothing else mattered, she heard his voice, muffled as though coming from some great distance.

"Keep me from remembering," she sobbed. "Help me blot out the past. I want to forget everything . . . everything but ourselves."

Starting as if he heard some ominous sound, he released her abruptly. Straightening, he turned his head over his shoulder and stood motionless in the silence of the voluminously draped chamber, listening.

"Strange," he mumbled at length, "that he hasn't come back yet. He's been gone all day." Then he forgot Ying Tsung. His eyes brightened as he caught sight of a pewter vase of long-stemmed roses on a table near. Stepping over to it, he gently drew one out and held it up before her radiant black eyes.

"A flower . . . life . . . warmth," she acknowledged, whispering passionately. "I want to go on . . . to feel . . . to love. I must go on. Live!" Taking the rose preciously with her slender fingers, she held it close to her delicately curved lips and breathed its fragrance. "The red rose—so fresh, so full, and so exquisite. Today in its glory," she murmured. And slowly, she returned it to him. "A beautiful thought of yours."

"*Mein Liebchen*, I shall keep this always," he whispered, crushing the flower to his nostrils. "Always! Like an indelible emblem branded within me. Forever—through eternity . . . like an immortal fragrance . . . a triumph . . . a symbol . . . a magnificent thought—in sweet remembrance of you, *mein Liebchen*." He pressed the rose into his pocket. She swayed toward him.

As she gave herself up to his embrace he bent closer

and closer, till the warm, fresh nearness of her body, the faint fragrance of her hair, like the sweet perfume of the honeysuckle, intoxicated him. Gently he brushed her silken hair with his lips. Fervently he pressed them against her white loveliness. Languidly her eyelids closed. A soothing faintness came over her. She felt herself yielding to his burning caresses.

The last remnant of his self-control shattered, he swept her up violently into his powerful arms. Her head fell back against his broad shoulder as he carried her, pale-lipped and trembling, toward the inner room. Her slender arms went out around him in mute appeal. He wrenched the curtains together.

~§~

The two speeding police cars swooped up to the curb and came to a stop. Under the command of Inspector Hogan, a squad of eleven heavy-set, stolid men climbed out onto the sidewalk.

Some of them, with tommy guns slung under their arms, the black pipe-like snouts protruding, joined the detachments of deployed men, and together they converged on Waverly Place, their black figures moving in coordinated units.

Shrieking sirens, piercing police whistles, clanging bells rent the stillness of the snow-blanketed park, rudely breaking the serenity of the somnolent square. Lights here and there in surrounding buildings suddenly went out, windows slid open, heads popped out. From the darkness people came running up from all directions.

Burly cops swinging clubs formed police lines. Hurrying men with white police cards stuck in their hats, some with cameras, passed importantly through the forming lines of surging onlookers. An open emergency wagon packed with men sitting erect, two standing on the back step clinging onto side rails, the bell rapidly clanging, rumbled into Waverly Place and stopped in front of the fourth house. Carrying hoods like diving helmets, some of them with cylindrical tanks strapped to their backs, the Emergency Squad piled out of the wagon.

His square jaw set, Inspector Hogan led the men up the steep steps into the dark vestibule. Two of the squad, with windowed hoods over their heads, stepped up to the opened Colonial door and knelt before the massive steel barrier. Men gripping their tommy guns hugged the sides of the narrow entrance.

A small yellow light at the end of two oxyacetylene torches flickered into a thin blue hissing flame; They applied the superheated torches along the sides of the steel door. Spluttering and popping, the flame grew to a dazzling green and ate into the steel. The reflection of the green dancing light against the weird hooded figures was like a fantastic picture, the conception of a surrealist.

~§~

The somber-lighted music room, with its pipe organ mounted at one end, the curtains before the adjoining room still tightly drawn, was deathly quiet except for an ominous sibilant noise which sounded faintly from the hallway.

Suddenly a deep, resounding thud like the dull plump of weighty bare feet striking abruptly upon the floor came from the inner chamber. The curtains were rudely parted. In his stocking feet and in a white shirt loomed the hairy, disheveled bulk of Dr. Schalkenbach. His shaggy hair fell away from his distorted face, his eyes blazed wildly, and his enormous lips curved in a savage snarl.

"You hag!" he bellowed insanely, tearing at his hair. "You hag! *Du Fliedermause!* You . . . !"

Like a man possessed of demons he bolted into the music room, followed by the hunched-over figure of a withered woman. With ashen-white hair straggling over her shrunken, livid, face, shaking convulsively, she hobbled across the room to the long mirror, an old woman. For a breathless moment, she stared in shuddering astonishment at herself. Then she turned and seized the vase of roses and hurled it violently at her hideous reflection. The thick plate glass smashed. Swooning, she fell upon the shattered glass and lay motionless.

At that moment, the heavy steel door crashed to the floor of the hall with a vibrant metallic thud. As Dr. Schalkenbach glimpsed the armed figure of a man crawling through the opening of the armor plate he whirled in his tracks and bounded out of the chamber, disappearing behind the draperies.

His service automatic drawn, Inspector Hogan fumbled with his left hand along the wall of the hall for the light switch and flicked it on. Leading a squad of five determined men carrying tommy guns tightly gripped in their hands, he advanced doggedly through the hallway and into the music room. In their wake Huxford, with Robert close at his heels, hurried to the prone body and stooped over it.

"Cynthia!" Robert called, bewildered.

The criminologist's eyes closed to a crack. He picked up his cane, faced Robert.

"Cynthia Winthrop is dead!"

~§~

Storming into the laboratory like a snorting bull Dr. Schalkenbach made his way stumbling between tables and racks of chemicals to a door near the row of glass compartments, slid a holt, and drew the door wide open.

Katherine Van Allen, startled, rose from the couch in the room in which she had been a prisoner. Her deep blue eyes widening in horror, her blonde hair falling over her blue negligee, she shrank from him in utter terror.

"I am going to give you your freedom, *mein Liebchen!*" he announced sarcastically, fixing her in a savage stare.

Then, seizing her by the wrist, he pulled her struggling into the laboratory. Gutturally he roared with sadistic pleasure as he took hold of an iron lever and shoved it down. The thick glass doors to his hat chambers rattled as they slid wide open. A tumultuous squeaking rose from the open compartments. There was a rustling noise, like the rapid flapping of many wings, and the black-webbed-winged mammals fluttered out into the room.

Katherine gave a piercing scream, her hands weaving furiously as the bloodthirsty vampires flew to relentless attack upon her white loveliness. Simultaneously, the cracking of splitting wood sounded. The Inspector's men were hastily chopping away the door that barred their entrance.

The crazed Dr. Schalkenbach floundered wildly through the room, upsetting apparatus and test tubes. White vapor rose in explosive puffs about the overturned tables.

He ran into a dark passageway.

In the stifling fumes, the bats flying in clusters about her, Katherine sank trembling to the stone floor. Her white throat and delicately curved shoulders were now helplessly exposed; the bloodsucking creatures, their bulldog faces wrinkled in a sneer, their fangs sticking out, alighted, drew nearer to her in slow, deliberate, wobbling movements by spreading their cloak-like forms and nudging along the floor with the "thumbs" of their wings.

The wooden barrier splintered to pieces. Inspector Hogan, followed by his squad and Huxford and Robert, hurtled over the smashed door into the vaporous chamber, his men scattering in all directions. Fighting his way through the swarming bats, Robert rushed to Katherine's side, lifted her in his arms. Staggering, he carried her from the laboratory.

Excited crowds jostled and pushed, held by menacing clubs. Sharp blasts of police whistles screamed above the tumult. Trucks with portable searchlights jockeyed into position, gears grinding, while uniformed crews with military precision elevated lights into the air. A mobile broadcasting unit moved up, the announcer speaking rapidly into the microphone from the open hatch in the roof.

Tumultuous shouting went up from the crowd. The glare of searchlights cut through the night, their powerful beams beginning to play over the darkened row of houses. The roar of fire engines rose above the clamor, a hook-and-ladder truck careened around the corner, brushing a crowd of scrambling humanity. The beam of a portable searchlight played down from the top of an overlooking building. The stubby barrels of guns poked out over the roof's stone parapet.

The searchlight's beam swept the tops of the houses, catching the white shirt of a massive figure emerging from the shadows of a roof below. The dazzling beam spotlighted Dr. Schalkenbach. He sprung and hid himself behind a tank. Flames blotched the night with red patches as the chatter of machine guns beat a relentless staccato. Bullets rang like the hammers of many gongs against the sides of the steel tank. Crouching, he hugged the shadows.

Schalkenbach straightened. Weaving his muscular arms over his head like a grizzly bear, he whirled away from the lank and leaped over a dividing wall and bounded from roof to roof.

As he reached the comer house overlooking Fifth Avenue, the beam again caught him. He threw his bulk behind a brick chimney. Jets of dancing Hames issued from the snout of a black projecting barrel. A machine gun loosed a jabbering burst of fire. Bullets sang in the air and thudded into the bricks.

With his powerful arms Dr. Schalkenbach grimly hugged the chimney. A tense lull followed. Again, the machine gun belched a chattering burst. Dr. Schalkenbach reeled. His enormous bulk fell and balanced against the coping of the roof, pivoted like a seesaw for a breathless moment. Then it swung out over the parapet and toppled, with an accompanying rumble of crumbling bricks, and dropped four stories to the street. With a sickening thud, in a rain of brick pellets his gargantuan body crashed in a heap upon the sidewalk. His clenched fist quivered open. The petals of a crushed rose scattered in the breeze. A glistening tear rolled down his rugged cheek.

As he fell, a cry of horror ran through the massed crowd. At that instant, the playing beam momentarily lighted the yellow-hued skin and slanted, coal-black eyes of a slight figure in the front rank of the crowd. Expressionless, Ying Tsung blinked.

"Even skillful doctor cannot cure himself . . . !"

Bruin Asylum

Make Your Reservations Today!

The Witching Night
C. S. Cody – Booking Now

A Garden Lost in Time
Jonathan Aycliffe – Booking Now

The Fungus
Harry Adam Knight – Booking Now

I Am Your Brother
G. S. Marlowe – Booking Now

Dr. Mabuse
Norbert Jacques – Booking Now

Walpole's Fantastic Tales, Volume I
Hugh Walpole – Booking Now

The Magician & Other Strange Stories
W. Somerset Maugham – Booking Now

The Bat Woman
Cromwell Gibbons – Booking now